She'd fought the ~~~~ when she'd enter~~~~

The alarm had been on, and Marlowe had thoroughly searched the place. But when he came back downstairs, she sensed a change in him. He kept his eyes on hers and his expression even.

It fascinated her how a stare could hypnotize her. She couldn't have dragged her eyes from his if she wanted to. Couldn't have stopped him from backing her into the corner and bracing his hands on either side of her head.

Good thing she didn't want to stop any part of this.

Desire balled in her stomach. Hunger clawed through her veins. Heat flowed over her skin. All from a mere touch.

He inclined his head slowly, still holding her gaze, but even when she felt his breath on her lips, he didn't kiss her. Instead, he wrapped his fingers around her nape and whispered the words she never wanted to hear.

"There's someone in the house."

paranoid feeling
ed the house.

JENNA RYAN

A PERFECT STRANGER

HARLEQUIN®

TORONTO • NEW YORK • LONDON
AMSTERDAM • PARIS • SYDNEY • HAMBURG
STOCKHOLM • ATHENS • TOKYO • MILAN • MADRID
PRAGUE • WARSAW • BUDAPEST • AUCKLAND

To the seven angels:
Sheena, Maya, Mystique, Salem, Serena,
Mandalay and Scarlett.
Love you all.

Recycling programs
for this product may
not exist in your area.

ISBN-13: 978-0-373-74503-6

A PERFECT STRANGER

Copyright © 2010 by Jacqueline Goff

ABOUT THE AUTHOR

Jenna Ryan started making up stories before she could read or write. Growing up, romance alone always had a strong appeal, but romantic suspense was the perfect fit. She tried out a number of different careers, including modeling, interior design and travel, but writing has always been her one true love. That and her longtime partner, Rod.

Inspired from book to book by her sister Kathy, she lives in a rural setting fifteen minutes from the city of Victoria, British Columbia. It's taken a lot of years, but she's finally slowed the frantic pace and adopted a West Coast mindset. Stay active, stay healthy, keep it simple. Enjoy the ride, enjoy the read. All of that works for her, but what she continues to enjoy most is writing stories she loves. She also loves reader feedback. E-mail her at jacquigoff@shaw.ca or visit Jenna Ryan on Facebook.

Books by Jenna Ryan

CAST OF CHARACTERS

Darcy Nolan—A photojournalist, she was forced to go into hiding after she helped send a drug lord to prison.

Damon Marlowe—The ex-cop turned P.I. has a dark past and no reason to care about the woman he's just exposed. But he does.

Vince Macos—With his father in prison, has the drug lord's son sent a killer after Darcy?

Valentino Reade—A Philadelphia cop in desperate need of money.

Elaine Holland—Darcy's editor wants that big story, and Darcy could be it.

Trace Grogan—Unpopular, untrustworthy and low, he works with and wants Darcy.

Hannah Brewster—She runs a boarding house and has more secrets than people might suspect.

Cristian Turner—Hannah's nephew arrived in town the day Darcy was first attacked.

John Hancock—The creepy boarding house tenant spends a lot of time watching Darcy.

Prologue

The police station smelled of sweat and stale coffee. It sounded like the bargain basement of a New York department store. And with the outdated central air-conditioning in desperate need of repair, it was hotter than the depths of hell.

Unruffled, photojournalist Shannon Hunt fanned her face with a discarded file folder and wondered how many stories could be ferreted out of this room by a canny fly-on-the-wall reporter. Dozens, she imagined, possibly more.

The amusement that tugged on her lips blossomed into a smile when Carmela Holden, a captain in Vice for thirty-plus years, strode through the door and barked her name.

"My office." She glared at the desk sergeant. "No interruptions."

Inside, Holden rounded her desk. "Dye your hair," she said without preface.

Shannon's brows went up. "Excuse me?"

The captain stared hard. "Dye it, cut it, buy a pair of glasses, sell your house."

"Condo. And again, excuse me?"

"Frankie Maco got twelve years in San Quentin."

"I know. I testified at the trial."

"Testified and were threatened."

"Very subtly, Captain, by a nephew who was high at the time."

"You didn't notice Frankie grinning like a Cheshire cat in the background?"

"What I saw was a grimace, probably of pain over his nephew's pathetic demeanor."

"A threat's a threat, to my mind. And twelve years doesn't cut it for me. I wanted twenty-five. He deserved that for the cocaine in his storehouse alone."

Shannon knew where this was going. She'd worked at a high-profile L.A. newsmagazine for the past eighteen months, had, in fact, contributed a good portion of the photo and video evidence that had set Frankie up. "Come on, Captain…" she began, but Holden slapped her palms on the desk.

"No, you come on, Hunt. I have a daughter

who reminds me so much of you it's almost scary. All you've got on her is ten years, a skull as thick as granite and the tenacity of her boyfriend's bull terrier."

Shannon crossed to the desk, planted her palms on it and met the woman's stare. "Flattery won't work, Carmela. I'd look ridiculous as a brunette, and I've done my homework. Frankie Maco's not a killer."

"That you know of."

"He's also not overly powerful beyond the city limits."

"That you know of."

"What I know is that he has a totally screwed-up family and a handful of street connections."

"Lots of screwed-up family and many street connections."

"He also has enemies and rivals and an arthritic mother he's taken care of for the past fifteen years."

"People around him have been known to disappear."

"And more than one of them has turned up again."

"Doesn't account for the dozen who haven't." Smoldering, Holden hit a key on her computer, swiveled the monitor. "I've got a new name for you, as well as a revamped portfolio and an altered family history. No more army brat. You'll be

Darcy Nolan, only child of Boston real estate agents Ann and Jerry Nolan. Your parents retired five years ago, died within eight months of each other. You've got an Irish-Swedish background, so go red with the hair and wear green contacts. I can have a job lined up for you in a day. Anywhere but here."

Shannon continued to stare, but there was no malice in it. How could she dislike a woman who had her safety at heart? "Your daughter's going to rebel, Holden."

"I'll deal with that if and when."

"I don't want to—"

"Think about it." The captain pinned her hand before she could draw away. "Really think about who and what Frankie Maco is. How he operates."

Shannon regarded her trapped fingers, then narrowed her eyes on the woman's face. "All right, I'll think. I'll even research his extended family. But I won't," she said with the barest trace of humor, "dye my hair. I'm a blonde and I'm staying that way."

"Best I could have hoped for." Releasing her, the captain shut off her monitor. "Watch your back, Hunt."

SHE WISHED HOLDEN hadn't said that because she'd been feeling twitchy ever since the trial ended. No, before that, actually. Facts were facts, however, and no one in or out of his organization had ever accused Frankie Maco of murder.

Of course, there was always that first time. And what Maco couldn't do from behind bars, his son, siblings or grandchildren might.

Shannon glanced in the rearview mirror. There was no one behind her on the exit ramp, no one trailing her along the dark street, and no one lying in wait when she reached her Tujunga Canyon home. She was letting Holden's fears get to her. And wouldn't her army-for-life parents just love to know that?

On the porch, a gust of hot, dry wind blew across her arms. Even her tank top felt like too much clothing in this ninety-five-degree weather. It made people cranky.

It made vice cops worry.

A bush rustled to her left. She caught a footstep, followed by a whiff of cologne, and managed a tight curse a split second before a large hand yanked her around and caught her throat in a choking, viselike grip.

Her head hit the condo door; her breath stalled in her lungs. A pair of black eyes bored into hers.

"You made a big mistake, lady," the man holding her growled. "I got a message for you."

She held herself dead still, returned his stare.

"Let go of me, Vince. You know very well Captain Holden has a pair of officers watching my place."

"Got here ahead of them, sugar. They're eating cold pizza, ogling your bedroom window and having dirty fantasies as we speak."

His grip tightened, and pinpricks of light began to appear before her eyes.

With her spine still pressed to the door, Shannon's hand traveled to the pocket of her jeans. Hooking the ring on the black box inside, she pulled it free.

A high-pitched shriek filled the air so that Vince clapped both palms to his ears.

"You won't know," he shouted above the deafening racket. "You won't see or hear. You won't expect. Cabdriver, store clerk, guy stuffing money in a parking meter. Someone, someday. Anyone, any day. Me being the most likely anyone of all. One clear shot, sugar. That's all I need. That's all I want."

Feet thudded on the stone walkway. Above her, a handful of windows flew open. Vince let a crooked grin steal across his lips before he ducked sideways out of the barely-there light.

The officers arrived, panting. One took off in pursuit, the other drew her aside.

He asked questions. Shannon responded. But

it was purely reflex. Only two things registered.
His partner wouldn't catch Frankie's slippery
son.

And Shannon Hunt was going to die.

Chapter One

New York City, 2009

The air was stinking hot. A stale breeze carried the muffled noise of human and street traffic. Bad music thumped above; a dog barked below. It was one of those New York nights when no one in the city slept.

There had been two brownouts in two days, and the forecast called for even higher temperatures tomorrow. The police chief was asking for the public's cooperation. Would he get it? Damon Marlowe had no idea, and he didn't care. Hadn't since leaving the force two years ago.

Somewhere in the shadows of his Soho studio, a tap dripped. The pipe that fed it rattled, and the walls groaned. If he listened hard enough, he might hear the 1970s wallpaper peeling.

Stretched out on his sofa, with a cold beer dangling between his fingers, he watched a cockroach crawl along a thin ceiling crack. He counted five, ten tops, a night—a decent average for the neighborhood. There'd been twice as many in his ex's Los Angeles apartment.

The memory brought a twinge, then suddenly, there it was—the smothering crush of grief, dulled by time but still a force to be reckoned with. Or locked away when he chose not to deal with it.

He opted for the lock and a deep pull on the bottle.

Behind him, his cell phone erupted into classic Eric Clapton. He listened for a moment, swirled his beer, then gave in and reached back.

"Marlowe," he said.

"Would that be Damon Marlowe of DM and Associates?"

He almost smiled at the man's polite tone. Slight European accent, perfect diction. Caller ID revealed a Southern California area code.

"Hours are nine to nine," he replied and raised the bottle to his lips. "It's three minutes to midnight here."

"I'll take that as a confirmation and say that I was referred to you by a former colleague, one who currently practices criminal law in Manhattan."

"Peter Duggan."

The caller seemed impressed. "So your reputation isn't exaggerated after all. Peter and I worked together in Los Angeles. My name is Umer Lugo. May I ask if you're engaged at the moment?"

Marlowe's lips curved into a faint smile. "I've got clients."

"Hardly unexpected. However, I've been authorized to offer you twice your usual rate, triple if you can finish what needs doing in under five days. I must warn you, though, I have little information about the party to be located."

Marlowe's humor, seldom stirred these days, kicked in. "This offer has a cloak-and-dagger ring to it, Mr. Lugo. As a former homicide cop, I prefer to drop the mystery and cut to the bottom line. Who do you want me to locate and why?"

"Three years ago, her name was Shannon Hunt. I have no clue what she calls herself today."

"Is there an outstanding warrant involved?"

"Nothing so dramatic, I'm afraid. The family simply wants her located and returned to the fold."

"How old is she?"

"Twenty-eight. Twenty-nine on Thanksgiving Day of this year. I can send you a photo, but it's possible she's altered her appearance."

Marlowe rolled the beaded bottle across his forehead. "Why?"

The lawyer sighed. "Are my reasons important?"

"If you want me to take the case, yeah."

"It's a matter of some delicacy. Shannon had a falling-out with a grandparent who recently lost his only other grandchild in a vehicular accident. When you're ninety-two, Mr. Marlowe, and your health is failing, you want to tie things up wherever possible and make amends. I'm sorry, but that's all the history I can give you. My practice is small but entirely reputable. Check me out if you wish. However, I would ask that you do so quickly. I'll need an answer by 6:00 a.m. your time."

Across the room, Marlowe's TV showed a carousel in motion. He saw a child's face fill with excitement as she clutched the golden pole.

Swinging his legs to the floor, he sat up, ran a hand through his hair. "Ninety-two, huh?"

"Unfortunately, I don't see ninety-three in the cards. Will you accept the job?"

Something in the man's tone set off a warning bell. Should he listen or not? Marlowe glanced at the TV screen, rocked his head from side to side. "Send me what you have. You check out, I'm on it."

"You're a good man, Mr. Marlowe."

A flicker of humor rose, dark and ominous. "Not good," he corrected. "Just a man."

Tossing the phone aside, he got up to snag the last cold beer.

"DARCY? ARE YOU THERE? For heaven's sake, answer. I've been leaving messages on your phone all day."

Elaine Holland sounded cranky, which was the last thing Darcy needed right then. "Radiator hose," she repeated to the baffled-looking man beside her with the wrench in his hand. She made a slicing motion. "It's split, leaking. Just take a look, okay?" She turned her attention back to the phone. "Sorry, Elaine, I haven't checked my messages today. My rental car broke down." Her eyes traveled around the weedy lot outside what might loosely be called a service station. "I, uh, might be a little late getting back."

The mechanic used the wrench to indicate a nearby goat, and Darcy got his message. He'd loan her the animal for a ride. She turned away. "I'm still in Nicaragua. Unfortunately, I don't know how to describe car parts in Spanish."

"So you're stranded."

"*Sí.*"

"Damn. Did you talk to Dr. Aquilina?"

"Talked to, got photos of, visited his lab and his

experimental farm. A world food shortage is imminent, in his opinion, but avoidable if we're willing to open our minds and our stomachs to worms, rye grass and something he calls 'cocoluna.' Chocolate from the moon. You don't want to know the details on that one." She thought about the feature article she was to write and the looming deadline. "Now, why have you been calling me all day?"

Her editor huffed. "A guy's been asking questions about you."

That got her attention. Leaving the mechanic to kick her tires, Darcy put some space between them. "What kind of questions?"

"Odd ones. The name Shannon came up, which meant nothing to me or anyone else at the magazine. But after a while and more than one chat, I realized he was looking for you. Is your middle name Shannon?"

"No." Darcy moved into the shade of the sagging station. "What did you tell him?"

"That you'd been here a little over a year, during which time our circulation has increased. I thought he was a cop at first, but turns out he's a P.I. So I asked myself, what would a P.I. want with my Darcy? That's when it hit me. You're a question mark, kiddo. A lovely person but a puzzle only partly solved. Your parents are dead, aren't they?"

"Yes." Darcy's gaze swept the choked, brown landscape. "What's his name?"

"Damon Marlowe."

Meant nothing. "And he looks like…?"

"The guy's hot. Tall, very lean, with dark, wavy hair that hasn't seen a pair of scissors for months. He's not slick or polished, and as far as I can tell, he shoots from the hip. A bit thin, but the muscles are there for sure. I thought artist when I saw him, then rocker, then cop. Would you believe he has gold eyes? You'd say hazel, but the frustrated novelist in me saw an amber-eyed Heathcliff."

Darcy couldn't visualize anyone she knew.

She made another precautionary sweep of the area. Except for the goat, a dog the size of a Shetland pony and the mechanic, whose upper body had vanished under her car, there was no sign of life. Even the weeds were wilting in the glare of the sun.

"I checked his credentials," Elaine said. "Marlowe's for real. He works out of New York."

And Darcy worked out of Philadelphia for the moment, but credentials could be faked and identities altered. "Did you tell him where I am?" she asked.

"Hard to do since I wouldn't know if you drew me a map. Look, just get the hell out of there before the freaky Dr. Aquilina stops experiment-

ing on worms and decides cannibalism's the way
to go."

In spite of herself, Darcy laughed.

Her editor made a considering sound. "Do you
have a cousin named Shannon? I thought you
said you did."

"No cousins."

"Evil twin?"

"I'm ending this call now, Elaine. Wish me
luck."

When he saw she was free, the mechanic waved
her over. He smiled broadly and indicated the
overheated engine.

"At least you're at the right end of the car."
Swatting at a persistent wasp, Darcy slid the cell
phone into her bag.

Then whirled around as a loud blast erupted
from inside the ramshackle building.

"THREE AND HALF DAYS." Umer Lugo handed
Marlowe a certified check, drawn on his legal
firm's Swiss account. "I'm pleased and impressed. She'll be back in Philadelphia on
Thursday, you say?"

"That's the word at the magazine."

"Then I thank you for your services. I'll handle
the matter from here." Lugo swept an arm around
the crowded Turkish restaurant he'd chosen for

their meeting. "Select anything you want from the menu and enjoy it at your leisure. I'll be in town until Ms. Nolan returns. Perhaps I'll relax while I wait. So many wonderful sights to see."

And while he wouldn't be seeing any of them, Marlowe thought the man talked a good game. Just not good enough to fool an ex-cop.

Not his concern, he decided, and shook the hand Lugo offered.

With the check stuffed in his pocket, he made a mental list of outstanding bills and calculated he might have enough left over for a trip to Chile. The Andes. Somewhere remote, where he didn't know a soul.

His phone, clipped to the waistband of his jeans, began playing Clapton. He checked the screen and saw the name of someone he hadn't heard from for years, not since they'd worked together in Los Angeles and again briefly in Chicago.

"Hey there, slugger." Regardless of the circumstances, Valentino Reade always sounded cheerful. "I heard you were in town. What's up?"

Propping his elbows on the table, Marlowe rubbed a tired eye. "According to your captain, no one in your division. Hell, Val," he said with a faint grin, "you punched an old woman in a bar."

"A cage-wrestling bar. We were making a bust. Things got out of hand."

The grin became a chuckle. "Word's out, and it's made its way to Manhattan. Blydon's got five of you on restricted duty."

"Nice to hear your voice, too, old friend. Look, I'm off duty in ninety minutes. You working?"

"Was." Guilt snaked through his system. He picked up a stained menu. "I thought about heading home tonight, but I might hang around for a few days instead."

"Are you hanging around for yourself or because of a woman?"

"None of your business."

"Hot woman, huh? I'm fascinated." He named a local bar. "I'll meet you at ten. If you get there first, ask for table ten. And bring money. I'm flat until Friday."

Marlowe shook his head as he ended the call. One thing about Val, no one was a stranger.

Someone pumped up the volume on an already loud Turkish folk song. No idea why that, coupled with the suffocating layers of heat, smoking incense and spicy food, should bring to mind a blue-eyed blonde he'd never met. But there she was, the woman he'd located, floating front and center in the haze across from him.

Picking up his glass of ouzo, he took a contemplative sip. And tried to figure out why a case that should be done refused to let his cop-trained senses rest in peace.

A BACKFIRING TRUCK.

If she'd been older, Darcy's heart would have stopped. Luckily, the only explosive device in the area had been an ancient Ford truck that had coughed and sputtered its way out of the rickety service bay, then died for good behind her rental car.

It hadn't been a promising sight.

Yet, here she was, Darcy reflected, at ten-twenty on a Thursday night, two cars, four flights and a cab ride later, home at last. She was still on alert, though, since no one but a P.I. sent by one of Frankie's brood would be asking questions about her.

She paid the cabdriver, then hoisted her laptop, shoulder bag and carry-on. Three years and one month had passed since Frankie Maco's trial. She'd lived incident-free in Chicago, Minneapolis and Dallas. She'd covered stories from London to Sydney to Shanghai. Beyond the fact that she hadn't liked the insect life in Australia, nothing really strange had happened.

Her cover had held in all those places and for all this time—until now.

"Darcy? Is that you? Oh, I'm so glad you're home."

Darcy halted as a woman clattered down the stairs of the old Victorian across the street. Hannah Brewster was a sight, right down to her flowered muumuu, her flip-flops and her clacking costume jewelry.

"I've got a package for you in my storage room." The older woman patted her heaving chest. "It's from Switzerland."

"That'll be my godmother. If I don't call her every month, she sends me a clock."

"Really?"

"It's Nana's quirky idea of a reminder." Darcy's conscience gave a tiny ping. "I, uh, have a lot of clocks."

Hannah waved that aside. "Count yourself lucky. My one and only clock is upstairs snoring, with his feet six inches from the AC unit. My husband, Eddie," she said at Darcy's puzzled expression. "He's a cuckoo clock. You name an upcoming sporting event, he'll tell you what time it's on. Poor dear lost his baseball buddies when three of our boarders moved out last month, but I'm slowly refilling the rooms. I took on a new one just yesterday."

Darcy slanted a look at her neighbor's darkened house. "Long-term or short?"

"Day-to-day, for the moment. But it costs more that way, so the arrangement could change. Dear?" She tapped Darcy's arm at her prolonged stare. "Are you all right? You know, jet lag can make people a bit loopy."

"I'm fine. What's your new boarder like?"

"His name's Hancock. He has an accent, though I can't pin it down. Possibly English. But he's not your type."

"I have a type?"

"You do, and Mr. Hancock isn't it. You need James Dean."

What she needed, Darcy reflected, were answers. For the life of her, however, she didn't see getting them tonight.

So she let it go and pulled her gaze from the boardinghouse. "I'll pick up my package tomorrow, Mrs. B. Does your new man who's not my type have a first name?"

"John."

John Hancock… Okay, a bit pat, but not necessarily suspicious. She shifted her bags. "Maybe I'm tired at that," she murmured. "Good luck renting your rooms."

"Thank you, dear, and welcome home." Hannah fluttered a hand as she recrossed the street. "Don't worry about the rent until Monday.

You're a wonderful tenant, and I'd hate to lose you."

Darcy gripped her suitcase and started along the sidewalk of what Hannah Brewster swore was the finest rental property in Philadelphia. All in all, it was probably fine enough. But when and if she ever settled, she wanted something simpler than turn-of-the-century American. Something modern, with lots of glass and hopefully no more worries about Frankie Maco and company.

A cat meowed from the bushes as she disengaged the alarm.

"I know, Podge, it's ridiculously hot."

She didn't see it coming, didn't hear a thing. One second she was about to go inside, the next she was crashing into a bed of purple dahlias. Something scratchy whipped across her eyes. Another softer cloth—saturated with chemicals, her brain warned—descended on her face.

Twisting sideways, she avoided it, and with her forearm knocked her attacker's hand away. His fist rapped against his mouth, and she heard him grunt.

Still squirming, she rammed the heel of her hand into the side of his head. She'd been aiming for his ear and from his reaction thought she might have hit it.

When he jerked back, her instincts took over.

Planting both hands on his chest, she shoved. It gave her the space she needed to work her leg out from under him.

He felt strong, but she couldn't see well enough to fix an age on him. Young or old, however, she knew a man's vulnerable spots, and she aimed for the one that would cripple him the fastest.

Did she make full contact? Her brain said no, yet a second later, he was gone, tackled sideways by something or someone else she couldn't see.

The wool strip that had partially covered her eyes lay on the ground beside her. The chloroformed cloth had vanished with her attacker.

She rolled out of the flower bed and onto the grass. It took a moment to steady her breathing, another to realize that there was no one in the tiny front yard except her and Hannah's long-haired cat.

"What the hell was that, Podge?" she demanded, pushing to her feet. She swayed slightly, but shook herself and scrambled to locate her cell.

She had her thumb on the key pad when a man's hand closed over hers and a low voice came into her ear.

"Let's leave the police out of this, Ms. Hunt."

Chapter Two

Darcy's blood pressure spiked, then slowly settled. This man was holding her, not choking her. Relaxing her muscles, she offered a pleasant, "Let me guess. Damon Marlowe?"

"I'm impressed."

"Don't be. Word travels at warp speed in my business. Uh, do you mind?"

For an answer, he released her and moved back half a step.

With a smile on her lips, Darcy faced him.

Gorgeous was her first, frankly surprised, thought. Elaine had been right. If the word *sexy* could take human form, Damon Marlowe would be it. She would have continued to marvel at his amazing, albeit shadowed, features, but she had a different agenda in mind.

Keeping her smile in place, she said, "You saved my life. Thank you for that."

He moved a shoulder. "No—"

The crack of her hand across his cheek cut him off.

It had to hurt, but given his profession, maybe he was accustomed to being slapped. He absorbed the strike with nothing more than a lift of his brow. "Feel better now?"

"No, but you deserved that and more." Darcy's eyes glittered. "You destroyed a cover that's held for three years. Apparently, you also lost whoever it was you tackled, so now I get to spend a sleepless night wondering who he was, why you felt the need to rush to my rescue and what you stand to gain from it. Do you know what you've done, Marlowe? Do you have any idea?"

"You want to take another swing, don't you?" he asked without rancor.

"Love to." Her lips curved. "Will you stand still and let me?"

"I might."

The answer was just unexpected enough to make her laugh. Then suspicion moved in and she circled him with caution. "Who hired you? Was it Vince?"

"Umer Lugo."

She stopped. "Who?"

"Not your dying, ninety-two-year-old grandfather's lawyer, I assume."

"My dying…" She shook the question away as

her thoughts slid in a more disturbing direction. "Where is he? The guy who jumped me?"

"He grabbed your neighbor's bike and took off. He was gone by the time I reached the corner."

Darcy released a frustrated breath. "Let me get this straight. Whether by accident or design, you sicced someone on me. Then you switched sides and ran him off. I'm an investigative reporter, Marlowe. Oh, but wait, you already know that. You also know my real name. You relayed my alias to Umer Lugo, who very likely relayed it to Frankie Maco. By rights, I should be dead, and you should be home counting your money. So tell me, Mr. New York P.I., why isn't the story playing like that?"

"You don't trust me."

"Last I checked, I was a sane American female. What's the deal? Why are you here?"

"Call it a rare attack of conscience, likely spawned by the fact that I was a cop in a former life. Losing the guy who jumped you pisses me off, but nowhere near as much as letting myself be set up."

"Frankie Maco's very good at setups. Do you know who Frankie is?"

"His mug shot made the rounds before I left the force."

"And there it is. You didn't do your homework. Umer came up clean, so you were good to go. Bet he paid you plenty, huh?"

"Enough. Look, Shannon—"

"Darcy." A false smile. "For what it's worth and what might be salvageable—probably not much—I've been Darcy Nolan for three years now. I prefer to keep as many doors closed and windows open as I can." When something rustled the bushes near the fence, she sighed. "Much as I hate to suggest this, we should probably finish our chat inside, where no one can come crashing through a hedgerow on a stolen bike. Can you imagine the headline? My editor would have the exclusive she's been longing for, followed by book and screenplay rights. All things good in her world."

Marlowe picked up her bags as she started for the stoop. "She's not a friend?"

"Oh, Elaine and I are friendly enough, but longings are longings, after all."

"You don't sound bitter."

"Bitterness is a destructive emotion. I prefer being positive."

"And you can find a shred of that here?"

She tossed a smile over her shoulder. "Of course I can. Three years, a name change and one late-night attack later, I'm still alive."

HE DIDN'T WANT TO step inside her home. Didn't want to know her, or anything more about her than was absolutely necessary. Simpler, smarter, easier to keep her at arm's length and think of her in two dimensions rather than three.

Unfortunately, it was too late for that, and the anger crawling in his belly wasn't the kind he could push away. He deposited her bags next to the door, then followed her down a wide corridor to the kitchen.

Shadows hung everywhere in the old house. They spilled over the upstairs railing and slashed through the carved wood of the banister, lengthened on the hardwood floors and darkened cream walls.

In the kitchen, she switched on the overhead light. "Here's the deal. You tell me what I deserve to know, and you can have a beer."

Unexpected amusement rippled through him. "I've given you the meat, Darcy, all true and more or less verifiable. Lugo called, said he'd been referred to me by a former client. The client vouched for him. Money was good, man came up clean, I took the case."

She headed for the fridge. "Tell me, were you this gullible as a cop?"

He gave a humorless laugh. "Goes hand in

hand with cynical, insensitive and don't give a rat's ass about other people."

"Sounds like burnout to me."

"Any way you look at it, I screwed up, and you're paying the price. You get killed, it'll be on my conscience."

"Well, hey, don't sugarcoat the possibilities."

"Do you want them sugarcoated?"

"What I want," she replied, "is Umer Lugo's phone number. I want to know who hired him. Because while I'm ninety-five percent sure one of Frankie Maco's family members is behind this, I've done other stories about a few other people who might not like some of the things I've said." She waved her hand. "A lot of stories, actually. Anyway, my point is that knowledge is the key, and the key in this case is one Umer Lugo."

The beer she tossed him was ice-cold and medium dark.

Marlowe let his gaze travel over her body. Shouldn't, but it wasn't as if he'd walked in unprepared.

She was pretty, all right. Beautiful, if you liked moonlight blondes with mile-long legs, sultry blue eyes and a killer smile. Her hair was straight, shoulder-length and made him think of silk. The edgy razor cut suited her. It was also the only noticeable change she'd made to her appearance since leaving L.A. three years ago.

"And now, he looks." She pushed off gracefully from the fridge. "Don't worry, Marlowe, I'm not going to seduce you. I only pull out the Mata Hari card when there's a chance it'll work. Guys who claim not to give a rat's ass about people aren't likely to succumb."

"You like positive, I like simple. Just so we're clear."

"As Mississippi mud. Now, about Lugo."

He twisted off the top, drank deeply. "He said he'd be staying in the city until you got back. That might or might not be true." Lowering the bottle, he asked, "Do you have a laptop?"

"You dropped it by the front door." She uncapped a bottle of orange juice. "Why would he hang around?" she mused. Then she considered. "How old is he?"

"Fifty-eight."

"Muscular and tall?"

"Five-six and stocky with a hump on his back."

"Charming. Do you have the name of his hotel?"

"Give me five minutes on your computer and I will."

She started toward him, dangerous in a way only a man on the edge would understand. "And then?"

Because he knew what she was thinking, he used the beer to cover a burgeoning smile. "Sorry to disappoint you, Darcy, but I've dealt with reporters before. I go in alone, you follow me. So we'll save time and do this together."

Setting her tongue on her upper lip, she tipped her head to the side, strolled closer and assessed him from top to bottom. "You're a man of mystery and surprise, Marlowe. I foresee all kinds of problems between us."

"I see them here and now."

Humor sparkled in her eyes. "You can drop the guard. I told you I wouldn't play the seduction card, and I meant it."

Was he on guard? Maybe. Probably. Didn't mean he had to ditch a rather intriguing situation. He just had to make sure he didn't get tangled up in it.

Taking another drink, he let his gaze slide over her face. "I'm not afraid of you."

The sparkle blossomed into a smile. "Oh, I believe that. Your kind isn't afraid of any woman."

"I'm a kind?"

"Very much so. You're immovable, inscrutable, emotionally distant, and if I were a female rat, I wouldn't even consider exposing my ass to you. Unfortunately, you're also hot and sexy, and I'm going to guess chockfull of bad-boy vices. Makes you irresistible to a female like me. Therefore—" letting a sly look steal across her face, she hooked her finger around the front of his T-shirt and gave a tug "—my feeling is, we should get this out of the way now, before we move on."

A thread of amusement, mostly dark, wove through his system. "I'm not a gentleman, Darcy."

"Well, I'm shocked."

Eyes glittering, he let the darkness have its way, set the bottle down and trapped her jaw between the fingers and thumb of his right hand.

"Lady, this is one mistake I'm going to enjoy." Leaving no time for second thoughts, he covered her mouth with his.

HE TASTED LIKE SOMETHING forbidden, something she should run from and not look back.

He went in deep, and he savored. He made light and color shimmer to life in her head. When he finally stepped back, it took several long moments for the drumbeat he'd created in her blood to subside.

Now that, she thought through a lovely warm haze, was a kiss.

He didn't say a word afterward, just stared into her eyes, then turned and walked out.

Darcy knew his mind was working. On what, she wasn't sure. But that was enigmatic for you.

He returned a moment later with her laptop. The haze vanished when he told her where Umer Lugo was staying.

It took them twenty-five minutes to reach their destination in Marlowe's Land Rover. During that time, Darcy rattled off a dozen questions, most of them concerning the state of Lugo's mental health.

"The Declaration Inn." She read the dimly lit sign from the parking lot off the westbound Interstate. "Aka the Bates Motel. I see five cars, three of them old and rusty, outside four doors. The only visible lights are in the lobby, and there's no one behind the desk."

Marlowe surveyed the low structure as they got out of the car.

"Question," she said as they navigated the ravaged lot. "Why do you suppose Lugo is staying in a place like this?"

With his fingers wrapped around her bare upper arm, Marlowe swept the line of doors. "I don't know." He glanced down when she turned her ankle. "You probably shouldn't have worn heels."

"If I'd known about this parking lot, I'd have worn combat boots." And full camo gear, she thought, although the pale pink dress that stopped just above her knees and crisscrossed in the back was definitely cooler. "I hope the manager isn't a weirded-out mama's boy." She peered through the spotty glass. "Still no one in sight."

"Easier for us to find Lugo's room and get inside."

"It's a fine line between cop and crook, isn't it?"

"Ex-cop."

"And the line gets finer."

The lobby door creaked, but no bell announced them. In fact, the only sound came from a pair of droning flies and a whiny Merle Haggard song emanating from the dusty wall speakers.

Steadier now on the cracked linoleum tiles, Darcy eased her arm free. In her mind, she was still going over a kiss that had left her breathless and oddly light-headed. At this moment, though, and given the circumstances, distance was more prudent.

She ran a finger down the open register while Marlowe checked out the shadowy back room. "There's someone named Jones in three," she told him. "A double *X* in eleven and a squiggly line with two big rabbit ears in five."

"Anything that looks like Lugo?" Marlowe asked from the inner door.

She ran the list. "Lucky number seven." Then she glanced at the Peg-Board. "There's no key."

Returning to the desk, Marlowe took her hand. "Let's go."

Drawing a gun she hadn't realized he was carrying from the waistband of his jeans, he nodded forward.

At the door of room seven she gave two firm taps. "Mr. Lugo? It's Darcy Nolan."

Five seconds ticked by. "Mr. Lugo?" she tried again. "Are you there?"

No light came on.

"Door's paper-thin," she noted. "Unless he sleeps with earplugs, I'd say he's— Oh, God, you're not. A credit card?"

Seconds later, Marlowe opened the door to an expanse of black, the smell of must and Rambo playing on a very old TV.

He located a tippy floor lamp. The low-watt bulb cast a long shadow over a pair of twin beds, an open bottle of Bordeaux and an unzipped suitcase.

Darcy swung in a slow circle. "Well, this is really icky. Even on the lam, Janet Leigh wouldn't have showered in a motel room that had splotchy walls and vermin in the once green carpet."

"There's a reason he chose this place," Marlowe told her. He switched on a second lamp.

It didn't help, only made it possible for Darcy to step over the more suspect stains.

Her eyes landed on the desk behind him. "Laptop."

With a gleam in his eyes, Marlowe opened it, leaving Darcy to search the bathroom.

Palms braced on either side of the computer, he scanned the screen. "There's something here."

"Mr. Lugo?" she called at the bathroom door. Reaching for the knob, she paused, then shrugged and went for it. "Mr. Lugo?"

The first thing she saw was a dirty window with just enough light trickling through to reveal yet another empty room. Still, she felt strangely deflated as she lifted the hair from her overheated neck. Whatever the man's program might be, his absence wouldn't help them uncover it.

"What's on his computer?" she called back.

"Looks like an unsent e-mail."

Humor speared through her when she spied the drawn shower curtain. "Bet it's filthy," she murmured. But she gave the thin plastic a tug anyway.

And felt her mind freeze.

The faucet wasn't running, but there was water in the tub.

"Looks like Lugo was working on a report for his client," Marlowe said from the other room.

The sound of his voice fractured her temporary paralysis. With her eyes on the bathtub, she backed toward the door. "Unless he brought someone with him, he won't be finishing it." The words wanted to stick, but she forced them out. "Lugo's dead, Marlowe. He's got a bullet hole the size of a quarter in the middle of his forehead."

Chapter Three

Darcy had seen death before in the Amazon rain forest. And all things considered, the circumstances had been much more grisly. But she hadn't expected Lugo to be there when she'd opened the curtain.

"Drink this, Darcy."

She felt something cold in her hand and, looking down, saw a bottle of mineral water.

"Thanks." From her perch on the bed, she regarded Marlowe, then the now-closed bathroom door. "I'm okay. Shocked, but not in shock. It's just…" The memory repeated in garish neon. "He's fully dressed, Marlowe. Shirt, pants, tie. And yet the only visible blood relates to the bathtub. So he was what? Running a bath when the killer came in? Killer forced him into the tub?"

"It's as good a theory as any. You're sure you didn't recognize him?"

"Positive. Believe me, I got a very good look at his face."

Crouched in front of her, Marlowe trapped her chin so he could bring her gaze in line with his. "I called a friend of mine, Darcy. He knows Lugo hired me to find you. His name's Val Reade."

A single brow winged up. "Reade, as in the detective who punched an elderly woman in a bar brawl?"

"There's a story attached to it, but yeah, that's him."

Another man's face superimposed itself over Lugo's. Light brown hair, a little curly, wholesome features. A faint smile appeared. "I was one of the reporters who cornered your friend after his disciplinary hearing. Wrong place, right time. Elaine needed two filler pages before deadline."

"Did you write the article?"

"I started to. I had another piece to do about a political scandal in Alabama, so Elaine filled in the missing pieces." The smile grew. "She's not as diplomatic as me when it comes to matters of dubious police behavior." A sigh rose when she looked at the bathroom door. "Frankie wasn't big on murdering people."

"Frankie's not in control now, Darcy." Marlowe ran his thumb over her jaw. "Are you okay here if I go back to the desk?"

"Marlowe, I'm an army brat. I've heard and seen true horror. This is—" she searched for a fitting word "—tidy by comparison." Standing with him, she sipped her water. "Tell me, do all P.I.s erase rules like this?" When he merely glanced at her en route to Lugo's computer, she took another drink. "Figured that."

As he tapped the keys, she circled the room, letting her mind return to the attack at her house. She wanted to lay the blame at Vince Maco's feet, but it was possible he'd hired someone to attack her so he could deal with Lugo.

She caught the distant wail of sirens and moved to the window. "You've got about ninety seconds before your ex-cronies arrive, Marlowe."

"Let me know when you see the lights."

The word *accomplice* sprang to mind, but she blocked it and rested a shoulder against the window frame. "Are you plucking out any clues as that information whizzes past?"

"Only the e-mail he didn't send. Recipient unknown, text incomplete."

"Sounds like he was interrupted. Or he thought the tub might be full and he went to check on the water level. What does it say?"

"That the target's been located and the end is imminent."

"Efficient, ominous, and more personal than he

knew." She thought for a moment while she watched the horizon. "It also shows he was doing his job, so why kill him? Vince is nasty, but as far as I know, he follows Daddy's instructions."

"As far as you know. Three years might change a person's attitude."

"I see headlights. Three sets, and another vehicle approaching from the opposite direction."

The tapping continued. With each click, Darcy pictured Lugo's face. With each click, the face came closer, grew clearer.

Pushing on her temples, she turned from the window. "The rules you're ignoring are going to get you arrested in a minute."

A man's voice reached them from outside. "M, it's Val."

One last series of taps as gravel crunched in the unpaved lot, and suddenly he was behind her.

Val Reade strode in ahead of six uniformed officers. His eyes flicked from Darcy to Marlowe, then back again in mild suspicion. "Why do I recognize you?"

"Disciplinary hearing, three months ago. I was one of the people firing questions at you."

His expression cleared. "Thank God. I was afraid I might have hit on you."

"And been rejected?"

"It's been known to happen on rare occasions."

His almost twinkling eyes moved to the man behind her. "Still in the tub?"

"Just as Darcy found him."

Val motioned to the uniforms. "How hot was the water?"

"Room temperature."

"Which borders on body temperature at the moment." Val ran a hand through his brown curls. "That'll hinder the medical examiner. Did you know him?" he asked Darcy.

"No."

"Any idea who he was working for?"

"Possibly Frankie Maco. But that's assumption, not fact," she added at a look from Marlowe. "Frankie's the only person I can think of who'd bear a grudge strong enough to send lawyers and P.I.s after me three years down the road."

"I'll check him out."

"You?" Surprised amusement colored Marlowe's tone. "The captain put you in charge of the case?"

Val scratched his neck. "The word *shorthanded* came up during his telephone tirade. For some reason, Blydon likes you. You called me, I called him, case is mine. Now, Darcy, you and I need to have a nice long talk."

"About the discovery of Umer Lugo's body, or the attack outside my home?"

He stopped scratching. "You were attacked?"

"Guy got away," Marlowe said. "On a bicycle."

"Has all the earmarks of a three-ring circus, doesn't it?" Darcy remarked. "Except for…" She indicated the bathroom.

"That's a big exception." Pulling out his notebook, Val cast a level look at Marlowe. "And given the outcome, I hate to think who else might wind up in the same condition."

HE'D MISSED HER. She'd been underneath him, pinned and struggling, ripe for the taking. Then, wham, she hadn't been, because Lugo's P.I. had decided to play hero. He'd ruined the perfect opportunity with a broadside tackle that had shocked, infuriated and freaking hurt.

He'd pay for the bruises he'd inflicted. He'd pay like the lawyer had paid, only not so easily, not without pain. Oh, yeah, shooting off vital body parts was starting to sound real good about now.

In the end, though, it was all about Shannon. No, wait, call her Darcy. Live the charade. Until the charade ended and life became death ever after.

"Gonna get you, Darcy doll," he promised.

Shaping his thumb and index finger into a gun, he aimed at the TV set in front of him. He grinned as he pulled the imaginary trigger.

Then he pulled out his iPod, popped in his earbuds and bopped to the music of The King.

NIGHT MELTED SLOWLY into day. Marlowe spent most of both sweltering in the Center City police station.

Lugo's laptop had been bagged and tagged. So had his suitcase and wallet. Pictures had been snapped, the body removed, the motel room taped. Forensics would be dusting and sweeping throughout the weekend, and both Lugo's paralegal and his ex-wife had been notified.

It was a police matter now. Legally, Marlowe knew he could wrap things up in Philadelphia early Saturday morning and be back in his office by mid-afternoon.

So why wasn't he blowing off what had the potential to become a complicated tangle of red tape, blurred lines and emotions he had no desire to awaken? Why wasn't he putting as much distance as possible between himself and a beautiful blue-eyed blonde who was bound to screw up the structure, the fabric and the dubious integrity of his not yet unscrewed life?

Because those questions were far too heavy to think about, let alone deal with, he spent another night at another bar with Val, a long one that ended with him collapsed on the sofa while Val snored and muttered on a cot across the room.

He let his friend sleep the next morning, made a stale pretzel and coffee work as breakfast and, ignoring a hangover the size of Texas, headed out to purge his mind of the few loose ends he'd neglected to mention to the police.

On the drive back from the Declaration Inn, Darcy had told him about a man named John Hancock. He'd recently taken a room at her neighbor's boardinghouse. Probably nothing to it, but the cop in him couldn't let it go without a cursory look.

Only a look, though, he promised himself as he worked his way through the vaguely seedy streets of Val's neighborhood to Darcy's southwest Philly home. A look, a chat, an unimpassioned goodbye. End of case.

As he parked, Marlowe took note of a sunburned man pushing a hand mower around the front lawn of Hannah Brewster's boardinghouse.

A woman and a somewhat older man sat on the shaded front porch. The woman, in an odd flowered muumuu, used her foot to rock the hanging swing while she waved a folding fan in front of her face.

Her eyes brightened when Marlowe took the stairs two at a time. "My goodness, someone has more energy than me this fine August morning." Elbowing her companion, she stood.

Marlowe kept his smile easy and leaned a hip against the railing.

Beside her, the forty-something man with the receding hairline offered a rather feral smile. "Glad to know you. I'm Hancock from Houston."

By way of northern England, unless Marlowe had his accents wrong. And he doubted that, since his mother came from southern Scotland.

"Hannah Brewster." The woman smiled broadly. "My husband Eddie's inside watching a ball game." Shielding her eyes, she peered through the bushes. "And that's Cristian, mowing the lawn. He's my cousin Arden from Oklahoma's middle boy." She patted her chest. "Arden died, oh, it must be fifteen years ago now. I feel terrible we couldn't make it to the funeral, but Eddie was laid off at the time, and we didn't dare borrow against our properties. As it is, we're down to three from four, two on this street and a much older one on Faldo Road." She used her fan to slap at a wasp. "Would you like some iced tea, Mr...?"

"Marlowe. No, thanks. This is a very nice house, Mrs. Brewster."

"Nice and expensive," she agreed. "And it's Hannah. If you're looking to rent a room, I have one left. Second floor, faces the garden. Oh, here he is, Arden's boy. Come out of the sun, Cristian. This is Marlowe. He might be taking our last room."

Cristian's mop of blond curls, his eager expression and his lanky build reminded Marlowe of Val. But then Val reminded him of pretty much every college quarterback he'd played against at Michigan State.

"My last name's Turner." The twenty-something man cast an uncertain glance at Hancock, whose garish smile was starting to distort his mouth. "I'm pleased to meet you."

Hannah beamed. "Cristian's a painter. He came to Philadelphia because of our thriving artistic community."

Cristian rubbed at a bump on his neck. "I think something bit me, Aunt Hannah."

"Well, you march right inside and put some ice on it." Moving his hair, she tutted. "Will you look at that ear. Today it was a mosquito. Ten years ago it was— What was it again, dear? A schnauzer?"

"Rottweiler." Cristian tugged on his ragged left earlobe. "Owner figured he was going for my earring. I think he was going for my throat."

"You should have kicked him." Hancock raised a leg, but lowered it at a stern look from Hannah.

"Gotta show it who's boss," he finished with a nasty grin.

"Yeah, right. Uh, where's the ointment, Aunt Hannah?"

"In the downstairs bathroom, dear. Oh, and would you mind calling for Eddie to open up the garden room as you go past the study?"

Hancock smirked at Marlowe. "Don't know how long you're planning to stay, but if you get wind of any openings for a short-order cook, you let me know. My specialty's a burger... Whoa there, Silver." He broke off mid-sentence to leer. "Who would that pretty little darlin' be?"

Hannah rapped him again with her fan. "You put your eyes straight back in their sockets, Mr. Hancock. That's Darcy. Now, she's sweet as can be, but the two of you would simply not be compatible."

Both Cristian, riveted on the threshold, and Hancock, whose mouth had curled back into that Grinch-like smile, watched her bend and stretch as she extracted three bags of groceries from her trunk.

Exasperated, Hannah shooed both men along, then smiled at Marlowe. "Do say the garden room will suit you. It's on the cool side of the house."

Annoyed that he'd wanted to do a great deal

more than move John Hancock along, Marlowe returned his attention to the woman in front of him.

"Darcy's a reporter," Hannah revealed with a sly expression. "Sadly, she had some trouble a few days ago. Poor dear was mugged right outside her front door. I feel somewhat responsible since I'd talked to her not five minutes earlier."

"You didn't see anyone?"

Catching his arm, Hannah brought him down to her level. "See those hedges? A body could be murdered on the far side, and no one would ever know about it. If only she'd screamed."

"Guess she didn't think of it."

"Fortunately, the man ran away, no real harm done. Cristian will be trimming those bushes down to waist height as soon as he gets his second wind. I'd ask Eddie to do it, but it's difficult to schedule outdoor chores between sporting events." She dismissed the matter and straightened. "Now about that room. Seeing as it's my last, and Eddie scored on one of his long-shot bets this past week, we might be able to negotiate the price down a tad. Say forty-five dollars a night from fifty?"

Marlowe glanced at Darcy's hedge. "Does that include breakfast?"

"Lunch, as well, if you want it." She held out her hand. "Do we have a deal?"

Big mistake, Marlowe's instincts warned. He felt the darkness rolling through him. But in the end, it was Darcy he saw, and Darcy he continued to see even as the carousel of his mind revolved.

And with the darkness still slithering through his head, he accepted her hand.

"THANK YOU, THANK YOU, thank you." On the threshold of Darcy's office, Elaine hugged an eleven-page printout to her chest. "You not only made deadline, but you also made the moon chocolate readable."

"Well, hey, what are sleepless nights for if not to draft and redraft feature articles?"

"Yeah, what's up with that?" Removing thick reading glasses, her editor, a tall, narrow-chested woman in her early fifties, came in to perch on the arm of the sofa. "Some pervert jumps you outside your front door, and I hear about it from a cop? Really, kiddo, there's such a thing as a telephone."

Keys and sunglasses in hand, Darcy checked her e-mail. "There was more to it than I could tell you."

"Like a dead man in a sleazy motel room?"

"I can't give you details, Elaine. You know how the system works."

"I also know how much attention you usually pay to that system." Elaine leaned forward. "Was it anyone you knew?"

"No comment." Darcy reached for her shoulder bag, popped the glam sunglasses on top of her head and started for the door. "At least not until Monday."

Elaine bared her teeth. "This is so annoying. We both know how this stuff sells, and you're shutting me out."

"All I want to shut right now is the door."

Reaching back inside, Darcy snagged Elaine's wrist. "Give me a break, okay? It's a thousand degrees today, my landlady's given me five casseroles that no one with half a brain would eat, and if you think the cops are keeping me apprised of the investigation, you're wrong." At the elevator bank, she pressed Down. "I answered questions, gave my statement, answered more questions, then went home and spent the rest of yesterday and most of last night refining an article you insisted had to be done by Monday. Be happy. It's only Saturday, and there it is, in your freshly manicured hands."

Elaine admired her fingernails as they boarded the elevator. "I got the works for my date tonight."

"Yeah? Are we talking hot stud at last?"

"So-so. He's the CEO of a cable station that aspires to rival CNN."

Darcy let her eyes sparkle. "Does personality enter the picture at all?"

Elaine's lips smiled, her eyes didn't. "I'm fifty-something, kiddo. I've been married twice and lost money both times. I want Ebenezer Scrooge this time. Rich and stingy—except when it comes to me. Barring that elusive miracle, I'll have to hope and pray our little newsmagazine can break a story that has our big Manhattan brothers scrambling to catch up."

"So that would be a no to the personality question."

On the street with the burn of the early-evening sun on her shoulders, Darcy let Elaine pull her to a stop. "Get me an exclusive, okay? The magazine needs it. Your coworkers need it. I need it."

"I'll do my best." Darcy tweaked her editor's collar. "In the meantime, go home, cool down, get ready for tonight. I'll see you Monday."

"I sincerely hope so."

It was the tone of her voice more than her words that echoed in Darcy's head.

Too revved to return home, she detoured to the gym, the wonderfully cool gym with the fitness instructor whose hot body paled next to the memory of a certain P.I. she was determined to run, punch or meditate out of her system.

Of course it didn't work, but then she didn't expect it to. Any man whose face haunted her patchy sleep wasn't likely to be blown off that easily.

After showering, she pulled on a pair of jeans and a white tank top, packed her gear and headed for home.

Her arrival was greeted by a barking dog and the lingering traces of a barbecue. Mrs. Brewster's cat, Hodgepodge, lay on his back on the sidewalk with his paws in the air. Overhead, a faint breeze rustled the neighborhood trees.

Crouching as she passed, Darcy tickled Podge's tummy and received a yawning meow in response.

She realized with a twinge that she'd forgotten to set her house alarm when she'd left today. Foolish? Yes. But on the plus side, the front hedge had been trimmed as promised, and there was still a glimmer of light in the sky.

Her cell phone rang while she was climbing the porch stairs.

She glanced at the screen. "Oh, good. Perfect." She flipped it open. "I thought you'd be long gone by now, Marlowe."

"Guess we both thought wrong."

"So are we talking choice here or police order?"

She imagined his faint smile. "You found the body, Darcy."

"After you got us into the motel room."

"What can I say? Val's captain's a fan."

"Which means you're staying by choice, then."

"A dead client in a bathtub isn't good enough reason to stay?"

She dropped her keys in a bowl, her purse and gym bag on a high-backed chair. "Aren't you the one who said he didn't give a rat's ass about anybody—what was it your friend called you— M?"

"Val can't get his tongue around my name after a few drinks. Calling me M is the simple solution."

"Your friend had more than a few drinks last night if the coat I saw on his tongue today was any indication. I'm going out on a limb here, Marlowe, but I'd speculate that Detective Reade has some serious issues in his life."

"And you know someone who doesn't?"

Removing the bush hat she'd bought in Sydney, she shook her hair. "Tell me, have you always lived on the dark side?"

"You ask a lot of questions, Darcy."

"To which you give very few answers."

Wedging the phone between her shoulder and ear, she reached into the cupboard. "I saw your Land Rover at Hannah Brewster's this morning. I'm sure she was delighted to talk and talk and talk to you, but I could have saved you the headache and told you she didn't see or hear a thing Thursday night. If she had, the guy who attacked me wouldn't have made it out of the yard."

"Thanks for that."

"No offense. She just goes into superhuman mode in times of trouble, which, frankly, I'm surprised she missed that night."

"She misses more than you think."

Darcy dropped three large ice cubes into a glass. "Sorry, I'll need a hint for that one. Has something else happened?" When he didn't answer, she frowned. "Marlowe?" Sighing, she opened the fridge. "Come on, it's too hot for games. What is it you know that I don't?"

"Look behind you, pretty lady. You're not alone."

Darcy's heart leaped into in her throat. Her fingers froze on the handle.

The voice hadn't come from her phone.

Chapter Four

Darcy realized who it was a split second before the heel of her hand snapped to his throat.

"You," she stated thirty minutes and a short, temper-cooling walk later, "really need to break that habit of yours."

A step behind her on the crowded street, Marlowe grinned. "I thought you weren't talking to me."

"I'm not. I'm projecting." She turned to walk backward on the sidewalk. "It's how I work off being mad."

"Would've been faster and easier if you'd just laid into me at your house."

"I still can, if it'll make you feel better. You've got the potential to be a great second-story man, Marlowe. I have a finicky lock on an obscure cellar door that doesn't even read like a door anymore, and you go all Sherlock Holmes on me and find it. Point made? No. You have to jimmy the thing, wait for me to come home and set me up with a phone call. If I'd had a knife in my hand at the time, you might not be enjoying this or any other night scene ever again."

His gold eyes tracked her past an open bakery and on through a collection of outdoor café tables. "Which says to me, my point still hasn't been made."

"No, I get it." She turned back to navigate a crosswalk. "One, I should always set my alarm. Two, I should replace any faulty locks. And three, since I didn't do any of those things, you decided to show me that what you managed to do with a minimum amount of effort, someone a whole lot more lethal could also do. I'm not arguing, Marlowe, and I won't make those mistakes again. So can we please move on and get a hoagie?"

"Sounds like— Careful." Reaching out when she turned to face him once again, he steered her around a man in a MEDIchair.

"You've gotten out of the habit, haven't you?" he asked as the doors opened on a neighborhood playhouse and a crowd of people rushed by. "You think nothing can hurt you in a crowd."

Darcy zeroed in on a cart that sold some of the best street food in the area. "I like people," she agreed. "I like watching them live their lives, doing the things I wanted to do when I was a kid, but couldn't because army kids are born transient. That's not a complaint. I learned a lot and experienced more. But sometimes I wonder what it would have been like to grow up somewhere and know the streets, the stores, my neighbors."

"You're a gypsy, Darcy. Were then, still are now."

"Old habits," she said with a smile. "From the cart she selected two hoagies and two bottles of locally brewed beer. She knew he was watching her and, still smiling, continued to walk. "I have no idea what you're thinking, unless it has to do with Umer Lugo's death and why I haven't mentioned it for the past thirty minutes."

"My guess? You've been over it a dozen times already. You're tapped out."

She bumped her shoulder into his arm. "I'm also still irked at you for pointing it out the way you did." Not to mention, she reflected, for a kiss she might never erase from her mind.

She held her pulse in check with a sip of cold beer, then felt it spike when he eased her around the side of an Italian restaurant and into the alley.

Setting bottles and wrappers aside, he ran a thumb over her lower lip. His eyes were unreadable as they stared into hers. "I could get distracted by you, Darcy."

"Tell me about it. But that's not good, is it? For

either of us. I have gypsy tendencies, you don't want to care. I'm not sure I see the point in pursuing something that has Shakespearean tragedy written all over it."

The ghost of a smile appeared. "That doesn't sound like the positive Darcy I met two nights ago."

"Sometimes she reverts."

"To Shannon?"

"To S.L. Hunt. That was the name on my Los Angeles byline. S.L. was… Well, I'll be kind and call her a little too focused, a little too career-driven."

"You wouldn't say ambitious?"

"No, ambition was Shannon Stone's arena. Stone is my mother's family name. I adopted it when I did on-air weather reports in Oregon. It was a small town, and I was just starting out, and I thought Stone sounded more ruthless than Hunt. Then it occurred to me that ruthless might not play well on TV. When I relocated to northern California, I became Shannon Hunt."

"You did on-air weather in northern California?"

"Actually, I anchored the six o'clock news. Bigger town, bigger market, and in the end, a good, strategic move." She rested her head against the warm stone wall, let her mind drift.

"I stayed for about a year, then got an offer from a Los Angeles media group and went with the better money. That's when S.L. Hunt was born."

His eyes swept over her face. "So you traded in live action for the printed word. Why?"

"I told you. Better money. I wasn't in it for the glamour, Marlowe. I wanted to get ahead. Be someone. Make a difference. Well, maybe that part came later, but hey, I was in Hollywood. I was twenty-four, free to choose, and my boss liked me."

"Yeah? How much 'like' are we talking here?"

"Lots. And her name was Michelle." She lifted a hand to his hair. "None of this really matters, Marlowe. I'm Darcy now, not Shannon or S.L. Yes, I'm career-minded, but I'm not so fixated that I can't see, think or feel anything else. These days I prefer different sights, better thoughts, more positive feelings." As if to underscore those words, she angled her mouth toward his.

"Darcy…"

Undeterred, she moved her hips against him. "I'm pretty sure you started this."

His gaze dropped to her mouth. "Guess I did."

Maybe the sparkle in her eyes challenged him. Or maybe she shifted her body just enough that temptation toppled resistance. All Darcy knew was that one minute she wanted to kiss him, and the next he was lowering his mouth to hers.

Something exploded inside her. Her body came alive. She ran her hands over his shoulders and around his neck, until her fingers fisted in his hair.

Pinpoints of light, like fireflies, raced through her head. When he took the kiss deeper, she met him halfway, let the greed inside her rule. She tasted and teased and, pushing them both to the edge, nipped his bottom lip.

She managed to drag her mouth away a heartbeat short of hopping up and wrapping her legs around him. But her eyes danced as she took one final satisfying bite.

"Clear enough answer for you, Marlowe?"

"Might be—if I could remember the question."

Pressing the tip of her finger to his chin, Darcy indulged in one last, long kiss. Then she stepped out of temptation's way and made herself take a deep breath.

"I have to tell you, Marlowe, I expected wow, not a fireworks display."

Picking up the remains of their dinner, Marlowe dumped them in a nearby bin. "Not to diminish the moment, Darcy, but this isn't why I stayed in Philadelphia."

"Because I understand, I'll keep my distance and simply ask what comes next. Case wise, that is."

Grinning a little, he took her hand and drew her back onto the busy street. "I went through the list of contacts in Lugo's e-mail with Val. There were approximately thirty names."

"You think Maco—or whoever—would be on Lugo's contact list?"

"No, but it's a place to start. No one's found his client list yet."

"I assume the police have searched his office."

"Office and home. My former client—his former partner—still vouches for him."

As the number of shops and restaurants around them began to dwindle, Darcy pointed to a park entrance across the street. "Come on. We can check out the painters' exhibit and the flea market. There's also a band shell, a carousel and, if we're lucky, a puppet show."

When he didn't respond, she sighed. "*Enterprise* to Captain Kirk. Are you still running swiped laptop info in that overactive brain of yours?"

He sent her a sideways glance. "For your information, it was Spock, not Kirk, who had the overactive brain."

"You don't give us Earthlings much credit, do you, Marlowe? The rise to captain in any field of endeavor takes a great deal of brainpower." She regarded him in profile. "As a point of interest, how high did you rise in yours?"

"Lieutenant in the homicide division."

There was a rough edge to his voice that intrigued her. Before she could question it, he gave a humorless laugh.

"Yeah, I was all about murder once. Gang related, random, premeditated, crimes of passion— you name it, I investigated it."

She tread carefully. "In New York?"

"New York, Chicago, L.A. That's where I met Val."

"You met Val in Los Angeles?" For some reason, a chill danced along her spine. She shook it off. Almost. "When was that, exactly?"

He gave her another shrewd sideways look. "I know what you're thinking, Darcy, but Val's a good cop. Screwed-up, sure, but that's a personal thing."

"Uh-huh, and no cop has ever sold out for personal reasons— She stopped herself and shot him an apologetic look. "That was totally out of line. He's your friend. You know him. I'm just looking for—well, anything, really. Give me another twenty-four hours, and I'll start questioning the principles of my godmother."

"Who's out of the running because…?"

She laughed. "To start with, Nana lives in Geneva. She fosters abused pets and troubled teens, and she's an ordained minister." Darcy turned away from the cluster of flea market tents where couples and families wandered. "Uh, Marlowe? There's a guy back there, wearing a Yankees cap. I think I saw him when we bought our hoagies."

"You did."

"Is he following us?"

"Let's keep walking and see. What's that flickering through the trees?"

Setting trepidation aside, she smiled. "Let's keep walking and see."

She noticed that he stayed half a step behind her now.

"I still think it's Frankie Maco who's after me," she said over her shoulder. "If it isn't, though, and someone else wants me dead, that might be an even creepier prospect."

"Beware the enemy you know. Beware more the enemy you don't."

"Well, there's a comforting cliché." She led him through a stand of chestnut and willow trees to the source of the flickering.

An amused brow rose. "An outdoor movie?"

"Like a mini drive-in, without the steamy car windows and bad sound."

As she spoke, the screen exploded with action. Guns blasted, bodies dropped, blood flowed. Darcy looked back, but saw nothing except shadows and trees.

As more gunfire erupted on-screen, she swore she heard a bullet zing past her ear. But that was impossible. Wasn't it?

Six feet ahead, a woman on a blanket jumped to her knees. More shots rang out, and this time, Darcy heard a thwack as a bullet hit bark.

She twisted her head. "Where—"

It was all she got out. A second later, she was on the ground with Marlowe on one knee beside her.

"Stay down," he ordered. His eyes scanned the deep areas of shadow beyond the screen.

A moment later, everything went crazy. Rapid gunfire burst from the speakers. Darcy couldn't distinguish between terrifying reality and clever Hollywood magic.

"There." Marlowe had already yanked his own gun from his waistband. He kissed the top of her head. "Don't move," he said and took off.

The woman who'd jumped up pivoted awkwardly. Several other people did the same.

A shot ricocheted off the tree behind her. The woman screamed. For a moment, Darcy met her terrified brown eyes.

Then the woman screamed again—and dropped like a rag doll to the ground.

MARLOWE CUT BETWEEN the shooter and Darcy. Two more shots flew by him, so close that he heard the air move as the bullets rushed past his head.

Grainy film light dissolved to black and the trees morphed into grotesque silhouettes. Marlowe's eyes adjusted. Adrenaline pumped through his veins.

Ahead and slightly to his right, a row of lights illuminated a narrow path. He spied the man in the Yankees cap and knew the man had spotted him.

Bringing his gun up, he fired. Missed. The man leaped out of the glow and pounded along a second path, presumably toward the heart of the park.

Marlowe concentrated on the burn in his shooting arm where the first bullet fired had grazed him. Better him than Darcy, he reflected. If blood was some kind of payback, he'd take it. Then he'd catch the bastard who'd pulled the trigger and dump his sorry ass on Val's doorstep.

It would be over. Another name change, another lifestyle shift, and Darcy would be safe. Val would be back in his captain's good graces, and Marlowe could return to Soho where he belonged.

He heard a grunt ahead and veered toward it. He was running blind, nothing to go on except sound.

No more bullets whizzed past, no more shadows stirred.

His only option was to stop. And wait. Listen.

Something rattled to his right. It didn't sound like keys or feet on a grate, but there was metal involved, and it struck a familiar chord.

Keeping his eyes in motion and his gun angled skyward, he moved forward.

The rattle reached him again. This time it didn't stop.

Whipping around, he saw a large, heavy object barreling toward him out of the darkness.

HE LEFT THE PATH TO run across the grass, swearing with every angry step. He'd hiccupped when he'd pulled the trigger. His muscles had gone spastic and he'd missed.

It was supposed to be simple. Sneak in, fire, fade to black. But it hadn't gone down like that.

He spied a shape ahead, moving like a turtle and pushing something with wheels. Was it a woman? Hard to tell, but whatever it was, it looked old and dirty.

Sorry, lady, he thought, but in the words of The King, I'm gonna leave you all shook up. No fear, though, it's for a good cause. Gotta get Darcy, shake her up, too. Gotta do what it takes to make the dream come true.

With a song thumping in his head, he moved to intercept the shape, frozen now on a rough patch of grass. She didn't know it, but for tonight at least, this filthy old woman was going to be his good-luck charm.

Chapter Five

"Someone shot at you Saturday night? Seriously?" Elaine stared at Darcy across her antique cherrywood desk. "Are you sure the bullet wasn't a stray?"

Although she wanted to pace, Darcy settled on the arm of the sofa. "I'm sure."

"Yes, but… Oh, crap." Elaine grimaced as someone approached her office. "I recognize those footsteps."

Darcy refused to laugh at her editor's expression. "Trace?"

"Wanna bet he heard about your little adventure?"

On cue, a gangly man in his mid-twenties threw the door open. "I heard you got shot."

When he set a hand on the back of the sofa, Darcy fought the urge to lean away.

"We're busy here, Trace," Elaine called out from her desk. "I suggest you go back to the art room and work on stunning me with some innovative concept for whatever issue you people are currently working on. Assuming you're actually working and not frittering away your time playing PartyPoker."

Ignoring Elaine's glare, Trace edged closer to Darcy. "Are you sure you're not hurt? I could, you know, come by your place later." He winked. "Give you a thorough going-over."

"Oh, God." Darcy hid the softly uttered words behind a smile and got ready to intercept his hand. "That's…thoughtful of you, Trace, but I have plans tonight."

"With a man," Elaine put in, then blanked her expression at Darcy's vexed look.

Darcy slid from the sofa. "I need coffee. Anyone else?"

"Nine's still my morning limit, kiddo." Elaine folded her arms while Trace struggled with an unbecoming blush.

It was one of those awkward life moments, Darcy reflected, closing the door behind her. She didn't want to go out with Trace, but she didn't want to hang around and watch Elaine grind him into dust, either. Especially when the grinding related to her.

At lunchtime on a sweltering August afternoon, the magazine offices were virtually devoid of workers. Given the circumstances, Darcy wished she'd joined the exodus. But who'd had time for food? Elaine had been on a rampage, and the morning had been a mad jumble of police questions, postponed interviews and, unfortunately, injury checks.

The first and most significant had been the bullet graze on Marlowe's bicep. Thankfully, not serious. The second involved a homeless woman who'd sprained her ankle and bumped her head when she'd attempted to stop someone from stealing her overstuffed shopping cart. The third was the woman watching the outdoor movie who'd fainted when she'd realized what was happening.

Darcy brewed a fresh pot of coffee and tried not to hear the conversation taking place across the room. But even with the door closed, Elaine came through loud and clear.

As always, she went straight for the throat.

"Unlike you, Trace, Darcy doesn't eat, sleep and breathe video games. Take the hint. She's not interested."

Trace bumped up the volume. "You might be my boss, Elaine, but that doesn't give you the right to insult me."

"It does when you burst into my office unbidden and unannounced."

Darcy could almost see the anger crackling in the air between them.

"You're saying I shouldn't care if she lives or dies?"

"I'm saying you should look at her and every other woman in this establishment as a coworker and nothing more."

A whiny note crept in. "I'm not a bad person, Elaine."

"Bad, no. Screwed up, yes."

"I'm not…"

Elaine's exasperation was unmistakable and made Darcy wince. "For God's sake, Trace, you shook your mother until her teeth nearly rattled out, then spent the rest of the night sobbing in a jail cell. Don't you crumple your face at me. You shook her because she went out with a man who wore a pin-striped suit and two gold rings. Somehow that made him a pimp in your eyes. I swear, if you weren't somewhat valuable to this magazine, you'd be long gone. Now get back to your cubbyhole and leave Darcy alone. She has enough problems without you adding to them."

When Trace emerged, he looked as if he wanted to do more than shake Elaine. But then his breath heaved out and his shoulders slumped. His footsteps slowed but because his focus was off, he didn't notice the door open and Marlowe come in. A collision was inevitable and had Trace fumbling to apologize. Until he realized it was a stranger. "Who are you?" he demanded belligerently.

Darcy snagged his arms. "Trace Grogan, Damon Marlowe." After the introduction she steered Trace out. "Deadline's looming, Trace, and lunch break ends in ten."

Clearly suspicious of the new arrival, Trace nevertheless let her bulldoze him into the corridor and point him toward the elevator bank.

As he plodded away, she shuddered in revulsion.

"He's got a record."

She nearly jumped at the sound of Marlowe's voice. "Who does?" Then she did a double take. "Trace? What did he do?" She knew his mother hadn't pressed charges after their incident.

Darcy set a palm on his chest. "Please tell me Trace isn't some crazed freak who might decide to go postal one day."

"Nothing quite so dramatic." Removing her hand, Marlowe ran a light thumb over her knuckles. "He assaulted a man at a picnic."

The lower half of her arm tingled. While the sensation fascinated her, she kept her focus. "I know he's volatile and really messed up, but I've never actually seen him challenge a man before."

"This particular man criticized a layout he did for an ad campaign."

"That must have been for a previous employer."

"He's had several. This was three back from the magazine."

"I'd like to say I'm surprised, but I'm not. Anything else?"

"The guy who got pounded happened to be involved with Grogan's cousin."

"Let me guess. The guy he assaulted was a cop, right?"

Marlowe shook his head. "CEO of a statewide fast-food chain. It's not the guy Grogan hit who's significant. It's the cousin."

She felt a sucker punch coming, but couldn't deflect it. "Who's the cousin, Marlowe?"

"Trace Grogan's cousin is your boss, Elaine."

TRACE AND ELAINE. COUSINS. The word *yuck* came to mind and stuck, even after three long hours of repeat interrogation at police headquarters.

Darcy spent most of the afternoon downtown. Which was probably a good thing, since it gave her time to absorb what Marlowe had told her.

Val and his partner went over her responses twice. They compared her description of the man with Marlowe's and that of several other witnesses. So far, he told her, only the homeless woman had refused to cooperate. She was now in a shelter.

With task one complete, he switched his attention to Umer Lugo's e-mail contact list. He rattled off twenty unfamiliar names and finished with a frustrated sigh. "I have a copy of the client list we obtained from Lugo's paralegal. We're still working with his laptop. Every damn file in it is encrypted."

"Cyber gold mines usually are." Darcy used her hand to cool her face as they returned to the larger room.

"Central air's on half power." Val wiped his forehead, rummaged through the clutter on his desk for a copy of Lugo's client list. "How about I swing by your place tonight, after you talk to Whistler's great-grandmother?"

"Her name's Matilda." And Val seemed to think she'd open up to Darcy.

To her right, a small man with a heavy beard called out past the officer hauling him. "S'at you, Marlowe?" He tried to wave his tattooed arms but he was cuffed. "Over here."

"Hey, Comet." Marlowe preceded Val's captain out of his office. "Decided to relocate, huh?"

"Wore out my welcome up north. No sweat. Food's better in Philly." He leered at Darcy. "Ladies aren't bad, either."

"Ignore him," Val said.

While Marlowe talked to Comet, Val rocked his head from side to side. "Man, I'm tired. You know, some days I'd sell my pension plan to do it all again. Marlowe, too, I'm betting, especially where Lisa's concerned."

Darcy's brows went up.

"Damn." Val waved his hands. "Forget I said that."

"I'm a journalist, Detective. No cat could be more curious." She let him sweat for a minute while she fanned her cheeks serenely with the printout. "Now come over here and tell me everything you know—" a smile blossomed "—about Comet."

THE LAND ROVER'S AC couldn't keep up with the record-breaking heat. Darcy plucked at her sleeveless cotton top and visualized cool waterfalls.

"You've gone quiet," Marlowe remarked. He was slouched down on the passenger side using a New York Giants cap to cover his face. "I thought you said you were used to driving four-by-fours."

She leaned an elbow on the window well, regarded him at an angle. "I am. And I'm being quiet because you closed your eyes as soon as we left the station, so I assumed you wanted to sleep."

"Contrary to popular belief, I can converse with my eyes closed."

"Oh, good." Her smile came fast and lethal. "Let's jump right in then, shall we? You have a friend who's an informant, another who's a serious alcoholic and a BFF wannabe in Val's cranky captain. You go out drinking until all hours with the alcoholic, closet yourself in a stuffy little office with the wannabe, and relive old times for forty minutes with an informant who'd sell his grandmother for a three-hour high. You do all that with them, and yet you won't tell me anything about a case that, technically, you have less right to be involved in than I do. If you didn't kiss like Casanova, I'd swear you prefer a man's company to a woman's."

If she was hoping to get a rise, she was disappointed. All he did was chuckle and make a slight head motion at the windshield. "Red light."

"I see it."

"You're pissed off at me, aren't you?"

"No… Yes… Maybe." She knit her brow. "I'm not sure. I think I just want you to talk to me."

"What do you call what we're doing?"

"I want you to share, Marlowe. Something of yourself and of this so-called police investigation." Hot and angry, she swiped at the AC control.

"It's already on High." He surprised her by trapping her hand and lacing his fingers through hers. "It isn't personal with Comet or Blydon or even most of the time with Val. We talk about guy things. Sports, cars, women."

"And criminals?"

"Like women talk about shoes."

She smiled, then sighed. "I'm being bitchy. I'm not sure why because it isn't as if I haven't encountered adversity before. I usually just roll with it." Slowing, she peered through the windshield. "This is it. Home sweet temporary home for Matilda."

Marlowe's gaze climbed the dirty brick structure of the homeless shelter. "I've seen better."

She slid out, tossed him the keys. "I've seen worse. It's all down to perception. This place has a holding area for shopping carts. A lot of street people like that." Dropping her sunglasses in place, she smiled. "You coming or staying?"

"How is she with ex-cops?"

"Don't know. Maybe we should have brought your friend Comet along as a buffer." She stepped over garbage spilling from a split bag, waved at the swarm of flies buzzing around it. "Stop looking at me, Marlowe. She wanted to come here."

Marlowe reached around her to push open the front door.

The potbellied man at the desk didn't look up

from his magazine. "You got a warrant?" he growled.

Darcy smiled. "Is that a prerequisite for all visitors?"

He raised his eyes, ran them over her twice, then asked, "Who do you want?"

"Matilda."

"Seventeen's her room, but it won't do you no good to go there. She's down in the hole with her cart."

"The hole?" Darcy repeated.

"Keep walking, hang a right outside. You'll see it."

All this, Darcy reflected, to talk to a woman who probably couldn't tell them anything more than they already knew.

She led the way down the corridor, then on through a trash-strewn alley to what had probably been an underground parking lot. A cloud scudded across the sun, and a gust of wind blew several used food wrappers into a miniature funnel at the entrance.

"Matilda?" she called into the shadows.

No one answered.

"Matilda?" she tried again. "It's Darcy Nolan. We talked on Sunday."

Still nothing. And no sound except for distant traffic noise, flies and a few muffled shouts.

"I'm not going to hurt you." She squinted into the dark. "I just want to talk to you about the man who grabbed your cart. He—" She broke off when her foot caught on something and nearly sent her sprawling.

Marlowe's hands on her waist prevented the fall.

Rebalancing, she pushed the hair from her cheeks. "Note to self. Always carry a flashlight."

"Or wear flat shoes."

"You're such a man." A cloud rolled in, accompanied by a low peal of thunder over the river. The garage suddenly turned eerie. "Matilda? The desk clerk told us you were here." Darcy glanced down as her foot hit something again. She stopped, bent low, crept forward. "Uh, Marlowe?"

He swore under his breath. "Don't touch her."

Darcy's heart pounded as an outline took shape on the concrete. The outline of an old woman lying in a puddle of blood.

Chapter Six

Darcy pressed her fingers to the pulse in Matilda's neck. "She's alive."

"Call it in." Marlowe made a circle of the area. It read more like a grotto than a parking lot. The light that had trickled in earlier was now being obliterated by clouds.

They hadn't heard a shot, but they had heard raised voices. Had they interrupted something?

He thought he spied a movement far ahead, was sure of it when he heard the slap of rubber soles on concrete.

"Can you handle this?" he asked Darcy.

She nodded, kept talking to the 911 operator.

He took off toward the rear exit. The guy had a fifty-yard head start, and he'd have memorized the escape routes.

For the second time in three days, all Marlowe had was sound to guide him. A door opened, and for a split second, the runner was visible. He shot through the opening and appeared to turn right.

By the time Marlowe got there, the guy was gone. But going right took him down a filthy alley to a street that ran parallel to the shelter.

He spotted him a block farther on. Darting into traffic, the man used his baseball cap to flag down a cabbie who had to slam on his brakes to avoid hitting him.

"Not safe yet, pal." Marlowe cut through a side alley to the cross street.

The cab was just turning the corner when Marlowe emerged. The vehicle was moving away from him, but he got close enough to note both vehicle and plate numbers.

Winded and thoroughly pissed off, he pulled up, grabbed his cell and dialed.

"Detective Reade."

"Seventh House Street Shelter," Marlowe told him. "Witness is down. Shooter escaped in a yellow cab." He repeated the vehicle and plate.

"Got it. I'm en route. Did you recognize the shooter? Was it the guy from the park?"

"Yeah, it was him." Marlowe gave the wall of a derelict apartment building a frustrated whack. "Round up the cabdriver. He'll confirm the description."

"This one's getting ugly," Val said. "Whoever's

after Darcy doesn't give a damn about human life. Is Maco that ruthless?"

Marlowe started to jog back. "Yeah, he's that ruthless. He's also been in and out of the hospital a dozen times over the past few months."

"We got that same information, but it's a slippery slope where doctors are involved. You think he's terminal?"

"Could be."

"Bet you also think this has gotten way too personal."

Marlowe pushed through a door that was suspended by a single rusty hinge. "I'm not going there, Val."

"Understood, and I'll back off, but you have to see this isn't the same as Lisa. Darcy's more than capable—"

Swearing, Marlowe cut the connection, jogged through the shadows toward the flashing lights of the ambulance.

The sirens were off, but he could still hear them in his head—the combined wail of police, fire and ambulance vehicles as they'd converged on the tarmac. Music played in the background. Children squealed. Machinery clanked.

He blocked it, picked Darcy out of the crowd and focused. If he slammed his injured arm into a concrete column with enough force, he could use the immediate pain to offset the deeper one.

But what, he wondered as his sights narrowed from ten people down to one, could he use to offset Darcy?

MATILDA WAS GOING TO live. The bullet hadn't hit any major organs. She'd lost a lot of blood, but that just made subduing her easier for the hospital staff.

Although it was dark when Darcy got home, she spotted Mrs. Brewster's nephew sitting on her landlady's stoop. He had an iPod in one hand, a sandwich in the other and a canvas pack plopped at his feet. He had charcoal smudges on his face.

She smiled and walked toward him. "You've either been sketching or sweeping a chimney."

He grinned. "I set up in the park today. But I don't think Aunt Hannah appreciates my abstract art. She said I should consider a different style of painting, and I can start with her houses. Specifically with your house. I'm supposed to walk around it and examine the trim. I said I'd do it after dinner because she said you were working tonight." He nodded at her hedge. "I cut the tops down another six inches this afternoon. Now everyone can see your front door."

"Yes, I noticed that. Thank you."

A black vehicle pulled in behind hers. "That'll be Marlowe. Do you want to come inside? I can give you something to wash that sandwich down."

"No, I'm good. But thanks." Cristian stopped. "I almost forgot. I saw a light on in your house when I got home. It went out, but with all the trouble, I figured you should know. Uh, hi," he said to Marlowe, who was pocketing his keys.

Marlowe held his hands out to the sides as the younger man disappeared into the boarding-house. "Was it something I said?"

Darcy piled her laptop, camera and three large research books in his arms. "He's just shy. You probably make him feel young and awkward."

"He's older than you are, Darcy." Ignoring her glare, Marlowe nudged her along the path. "Yes, I checked him out."

"You investigated Mrs. Brewster's nephew?"

"He just happened to show up on her doorstep the day before you got back from Central America."

"Which naturally makes him a hit man." She shook her head. "Cristian doesn't look anything like the man in the Yankees cap. That guy is or was a boxer. I saw a nose that had been broken several times and a major cauliflower ear. Cauliflower," she repeated. "Not dog-bitten."

"Would you rather be cautious or dead?"

She disengaged the alarm. Marlowe had a point. Not that she'd admit it. Instead, she changed the subject. "I went through the names Val gave me this afternoon. I didn't recognize any of them."

With his free hand, Marlowe helped her push on the stuck door. "That's the client list Lugo's paralegal gave him. My guess is there'll be some different names in Lugo's laptop."

"Clients who paid him under the table?"

"It's been done before."

"I know." She paused with her finger on the light switch, shook off a twinge of nerves.

"Something?" Marlowe asked.

"The seeds of paranoia, if I'm not careful." She rescued her laptop and camera before they hit the floor. "Cristian thought he saw a light on over here when he got home. I don't know when that was or where he saw it…" She sighed when he pulled out his gun from the back of his jeans. "And you're going to look, aren't you?"

He arched a brow at the staircase. "Bedrooms?"

"Is that a question or a suggestion?"

The gleam in his eyes heated more than her skin. "Both, but in that order."

"Marlowe, the alarm was on when we came in. Would an intruder have thought to rearm it?"

"If the plan was to blindside you, yes."

He was going to go through every room, so she might as well accept it. And truthfully, she'd feel better knowing the house was empty.

It took him twenty minutes to inspect all the corners, closets and cubbyholes. In the basement, Darcy rested a shoulder on the wall and watched the cobwebs flutter.

"Have you ever owned a home before?" she asked when he reappeared.

"No." With one last sweep of the shadows, he shoved the gun under his shirt. "Why?"

"Curiosity, mostly. You're an enigma to me, Marlowe. I'm piecing your character together."

"You'll find you're missing a few pieces."

"I'm sure I'll find lots of things. So far, I can see you've got baggage. Easy read there. You were a good cop. Also easy. You don't want to care about people, but you do, which annoys you because you think not caring should be easy. Why, I'm not sure. Some sort of trauma or bad experience, I assume."

She started up the stairs, aware that she was pushing more than she should. But she wanted to understand him.

She turned at the top. "I can hear your teeth grinding from here. You're thinking that who you are is none of my business, that if you wanted me to know you'd tell me. My rebuttal is, if I wanted to know and didn't care enough to tell you to your face, I could ferret out the details on my own. I'm an investigative journalist. Ferreting's what I do, and details are my specialty. Ask Frankie Maco."

Because she wanted to gauge his reaction before she crossed too many lines, she walked backward as she spoke.

He kept his eyes on hers and his expression even. Old houses had shadows, and he used the ones in hers to maximum advantage. He didn't speak until she'd backed herself quite literally into a corner of her kitchen.

A faint smile tugged on his lips. "You talk a good game, Darcy, but I know when I'm being prodded."

She smiled. "And here I thought I was being subtle."

"Did you?"

She couldn't have dragged her eyes from his if she wanted to. Couldn't have stopped him from trapping her in the corner, with his hands braced on either side of her head and his lower body pressed into hers.

Good thing she didn't want to stop any part of this.

He inclined his head slowly, still holding her gaze. He had the most incredible aura about him, something that went deeper than his looks.

Desire balled in Darcy's stomach, hunger

clawed through it. Heat flowed over her skin. All that from a mere touch. Imagine what sex would be like.

When he still didn't kiss her, she ran a light finger across his chin. "You're fighting yourself way too much, Marlowe. It's a kiss, not a lifetime commitment."

She felt his breath on her lips and considered taking the first bite. She would have if she hadn't sensed something stronger than hesitation. "You know, you're not exactly feeding my ego."

To her surprise, he wrapped his fingers around her nape, gave her a quick kiss and murmured, "There's someone here."

Tuning in, she listened. A silent moment later, she shook her head. "What did you hear?"

"Something upstairs."

"Old houses—" A protracted creak halted her.

"Rear staircase?" Marlowe drew his gun.

She indicated a closed door. "The hinges need oiling, and the fifth and the tenth steps squeak." When he started toward it, she snagged his T-shirt. "I'm coming with you."

He regarded her for a moment, but stood aside and let her ease the door open.

The stairs were steep and narrow. They emerged at the end of the second-floor hallway, less than five feet from her bedroom.

Was the shooter inside with a gun aimed at the door?

Taking her by the shoulders, Marlowe set her against the wall. "Stay there."

Returning his attention to the door, he sized up the wood, gave the knob a twist and the edge a hard kick.

Darcy expected something—bullets or a body—to fly out of the darkness. What she got was another creak, this one from inside the closet.

She regarded the second door. "Okay, that's weird."

"Window's open."

"Yes, I see that." She set a hand on the knob.

"One quick yank," he told her.

She counted down from three. Pulled. Waited. Then watched in baffled silence as Marlowe slowly lowered his arms.

Unsure, she peered around the edge.

And for the second time that day found herself looking at a woman's body on the floor.

"Mrs. B?"

The woman inside had her legs drawn up and her arms wrapped tightly around her knees. She offered them a wide smile. "Hello, dear."

It was one of those rare occasions when Marlowe had to work at hiding his amusement.

Darcy simply stared. "You're in my closet."

Hannah's smile faltered. "Yes, I am."

"Why?"

The older woman extended a hand to Marlowe. "Can you help me? Thank you." Regaining her feet, she smoothed her muumuu. "The thing is, Darcy dear, I thought you were a burglar."

"A burglar."

"We've had break-ins in the neighborhood. Not recently, but at Christmastime. You might have been in Bermuda about then. Oh, I've always wanted to go—"

"What are you doing here, Hannah?" Marlowe interrupted.

She set a hand on her collarbone. "Well, I was—I came to water Darcy's plants, of course."

"My plants," Darcy repeated. "But I'm not out of town."

"Not now, no. I just thought it would help if I kept doing what I'd been doing while you were in Central America."

"That's, uh, very nice of you."

"You see, I thought you were working tonight. That's why I came when I did. Everything was fine until I heard noises downstairs. Well, I couldn't know it was you, so naturally, I hid."

Marlowe set a shoulder on the wall. "We

searched the closets, Hannah. You weren't in this one when we came up the first time."

"No, I wasn't. I was—" she started to gesture, but withdrew her hand "—somewhere else."

"We went through the whole house when we got back," Darcy said. "Attic to cellar."

A long breath rushed out. "It's an old house, dear. There's a room, a small one, between the master here and the stairwell."

"You mean a hidden room, with, like, a secret panel?"

Darcy sounded delighted, Marlowe not so much. "Where is it?" He steered Hannah toward the door. "Show me."

"It's not large," she insisted. "No more than five feet by four, and heaven knows, I have no idea what it was used for." In the corridor, she ran her fingers along the chair rail before pressing upward on the wood. A thin section separated to reveal a space with nothing in it except dust.

"I waited until I thought you—or rather the burglar—was gone, then I came out. I was trying to leave when I realized there was still someone here. I didn't know what to do, so I waited. When you started coming up the stairs, I ran into Darcy's closet."

"Well, there." Darcy brought her hands together, looked from Marlowe to Hannah.

"Mystery solved. You were doing a good deed, and it turned into a comedy of errors."

"Exactly." Hannah seemed relieved. "I'm so glad you understand. Oh, but it must be late. Eddie will be wondering where I am. He sometimes ventures out of his cave during the seventh-inning stretch." She headed down the hall with a backward wave. "I'll let myself out. You carry on as if none of this happened. And have no fear, your plants will never die of thirst while I'm around."

Darcy watched her go with more tolerance than Marlowe. He gave her an appraising look as she disappeared down the main staircase.

"Any of that story work for you?" he asked.

"Well, she does water my plants when I'm away. And she owns the house, so she has a key. There are a couple things, though."

"Like the open window?"

"For one. I never leave windows open when I'm not home."

Taking his hand, she drew him back into her bedroom with its muslin curtains, its large sleigh bed and even larger oak armoire.

In the middle of the floor, she executed a full circle. "Look around, Marlowe. Do you see plants in here? Clocks yes, plants no. In fact, you won't find a plant anywhere upstairs. I put them in the solarium when I went to Paris last April, and never brought them back up."

"Does Hannah know that?"

"Pretty sure she does. I've gone away about six times since then. And that's not the only riddle." Turning him ninety degrees as she passed, Darcy walked to the open closet. "I have a lot of accessories—shoes, belts, hats, purses—and I keep most of them in here. But this is something I've never owned." Bending to scoop an object off the floor, she draped it over her hand. "I believe," she said serenely, "this is called a garrote."

THE STARS WERE WINKING at him as he worked through his agitation by the river.

Voices bounced in his head like rubber balls. They grew louder, became a cacophony of useless words and stupid advice. Nothing he wanted to hear.

So he glowered at the river and pictured a pair of faces as if they were trapped inside TV screens. Buoyed by the idea, he aimed his imaginary gun. Oh, yeah. Now this was acting out.

He popped the P.I., right between the eyes. Watched him bleed, enjoyed it. As for the Darcy doll...

"It's just you and me, babe," he drawled in The King's Tennessee accent. "We're gonna do it up right when I get you by your pretty self. I can feel the burn already. We're going down, honey. Just like the man, you and me are gonna leave the building."

Slam-bang finish. Concert done.

Chapter Seven

Marlowe spent the night on Darcy's living room sofa. It wasn't where he wanted to be, just where he needed to stay if he had a hope in hell of resisting temptation. She'd offered him her guest room, but that was too close. He needed separation and for her not to wake up until he toppled into a more familiar nightmare.

He didn't expect to see headlights outside the window at 2:00 a.m., but his Clapton ring tone never surprised.

"Is that you out there, Val?" Dropping back, he studied his laptop, typed another word into the coded box.

His friend chuckled. "Man, you define the word *insomnia*. Okay to come in, or does your boardinghouse have a 'no visitors after midnight' policy?"

"I'm not at the boardinghouse. I'm at Darcy's."

"What? Oh, man, I'm sorry. I didn't… Why did you pick up?"

"Because I'm sitting on her couch, getting a migraine trying to break into Lugo's files."

"Is the front door open?"

"It will be."

The six-pack Val deposited on the coffee table was ice-cold and pearling. "Any luck?"

"I found Lugo's tax return for last year."

"He stored that in his laptop? Hell, I download a few raunchy pics, then worry all night that some joker in Internal Affairs will get his paws on them and blab to Blyden."

"Raunch isn't illegal. Lugo's tax return was."

"By how much?"

"Five, six hundred K. That's after a talk with his former partner and still no off-the-record client list. The number could go higher."

Val sat back. "Six hundred thou's not an outrageous amount considering some of the cases he's taken on."

"He has two Swiss bank accounts and a third in Costa Rica."

Val raised a beer can. "Any balances?"

"Not yet." Because he was hot and his mind kept going upstairs, Marlowe reached for one of the cans. "I should be able to do this. Get into Lugo's head and his computer."

Val's grin was slightly lopsided, his words

somewhat slurred. "Homicide was your specialty, not hacking."

"I was crap in Homicide." His gaze slid to the staircase before he dragged it back. "Did the cab-driver come through with a description?"

"It matches yours and Darcy's, but still doesn't take us anywhere."

"Where'd he go?"

"Independence Mall. Guy paid, hopped out, disappeared into the crowd."

"Any fingerprints?"

"Only about ten thousand, from door handle to seat belt. We're running them, but there were twice as many smudges that won't translate into anything, so I'm not holding my breath."

"What about that strip of blanket he used on Darcy during the first attack?"

"Nothing you wouldn't expect." Val started to drink, but paused and followed Marlowe's eyes to the stairs. "You, uh, think she's the type to settle down?"

"Doubt it."

"Could be she'll change her mind if she's right about Maco. Erase son Vince from the picture, old Frankie expires in a few months, and in slides a lower-profile nephew or niece to take the reins. Vendetta dies."

"Sounds good." Marlowe swallowed a mouthful of beer. "If it's a Maco who's after her. She's done a lot of controversial stories, Val, ruffled more than a few powerful feathers."

"Whose business and personal nests we've been taking apart twig by twig. So far we're batting zero. She's done some damage, sure, but nothing a good PR team couldn't spin back into place. Darcy reports facts. There's no malice involved."

While Val's remarks made sense, they didn't solve the problem. And they sure as hell didn't explain the discovery of a garrote in Darcy's closet.

Val polished off the six-pack, then slumped into an awkward sideways position and started snoring. Because of that, Marlowe didn't hear Darcy come down the stairs or realize she was there until he caught a glimpse of leg.

His eyes slid from knee to thigh. For the sake of his sanity, he stopped them there.

He needed something to relieve the sudden dryness in his throat, but with the beer long gone, he could only force his gaze back to the screen. "Why are you up, Darcy?"

"Hello to you, too." She moved, and he heard a faint swish of fabric. Silk? "I'm up because my mind refuses to shut down for more than an hour at a time. When it does, it spins in crazy sleep circles that result in even crazier dreams."

Marlowe struggled with an old image that had recently taken a new twist. "You could try sleeping pills."

"I could try beer, too." She nudged Val's ankle with her bare foot. "Like Detective Reade here."

Marlowe didn't look over. "He's off duty."

"I don't mean to judge, but don't you think he needs help?"

"We all need that, Darcy. Val knows he has a problem. He'll deal with it when he's ready."

"So shut up and go back to bed."

He skimmed through another file. "My mother swears by warm milk."

She reached out to play with his hair. "Maybe it's you who needs warm milk. Why the black mood?"

He supposed it could be the barely-there red silk robe. Or that her legs went on forever. Or that the scent she wore made him think of sex in a Moroccan bazaar.

Locking down his hormones, he continued to tap keys. "She doesn't have a record."

"If you mean Mrs. B, did you expect her to?"

"I never expect. I only investigate."

"I realize how it looks, but it wasn't necessarily Hannah who left the garrote in my closet. On the other hand, I'd rather it was her than a stranger."

"That's not very likely, Darcy."

"I'd have said the same thing about you having a mother." When he didn't respond, she bumped his arm. "Oh, come on, Marlowe. Tear yourself away from that thing for five minutes and relax. Your brain needs a break."

So did another part of him. Setting an elbow on his knee, he ran the side of his hand over his upper lip while he searched. "Go upstairs, Darcy. I'm not ready for this, and I don't think you are, either."

Another sigh escaped. "Maybe not." She glanced at Val. "Is he okay there?"

"Better there than behind the wheel." Marlowe shifted in an effort to ease his cramped muscles. Although he still didn't look, he relented a little. "She lives in Palm Springs with my father. He's a cosmetic surgeon. She's a surgical nurse in a different field. She's never had a cosmetic stitch in her life, and doesn't plan to. My father holds her up to his undecided patients as the perfect example of a woman transitioning gracefully through life's seasons."

"Really." Delight colored Darcy's tone. "I think I'd like your parents."

"You would." He scrolled down. "They're good people, with busy, active lives. They gave me a lot of slack growing up. Explore, discover, explore more—that's their philosophy. Mine's a little different."

"Yes, something about a rat's ass springs to mind. But I'll give you a break there, because— well, because I'm surprised and pleased you told me anything at all."

"They have a…" But something on the screen had him trailing off as he zeroed in.

"Marlowe?"

A slow smile formed on his lips and deepened as he took in the display. "Come to Papa."

Darcy angled closer to look. "Did you—My God, you did! You accessed Lugo's private client list."

DARCY'S HAIR WAS STILL damp when she dropped her gear on the sofa and shot straight to her office desk.

"Come on," she urged her computer. "Boot up."

Marlowe cracked open the adjoining door. "Who works here?"

"No one right now. Elaine's been told to downsize, so when one of the reporters quit, she didn't replace him. If our circulation keeps improving… Oh, come on, sweetheart, boot up." She gave the reluctant modem an encouraging pat. "New equipment wouldn't hurt, that's for sure."

"What time is it?" Marlowe asked.

"Security doesn't let anyone in the building until 6:00 a.m."

"So we're alone."

"Well, yeah. Would you come to work at this hour if you didn't have to?"

"Darcy?" As if cued, a voice reached them from the corridor. "Is that you?"

"Okay, you might if you were Elaine. Yes, it's me," Darcy called back. "I need something from the archives."

"At six in the morning?" A tall woman with short, dark hair and a pair of glasses sitting on top of her head strode in. "You're never here at this hour. Hello, Mr. Marlowe. I thought you must be Trace."

Darcy's finger hovered above the mouse. "You expected to find Trace in my office?"

"In any office. He's not particular whose space he invades. He just makes sure to do it in the wee hours of the morning."

"And you let him?"

"No, I don't let him. Why do you think I'm here? Speaking of." She whipped her glasses off and swung them between her and Marlowe. "No problem if this leads to a circulation-boosting exclusive. Otherwise, I wouldn't say no to an explanation."

"I did a story when I first came to the magazine." Darcy clicked, scrolled. "About a singer from Tennessee."

"Nelda Hickey. She's dead."

"I know. She overdosed three days before our October issue hit the stands—with her story prominently featured inside."

"That was a lucky coincidence." Elaine tossed a look in Marlowe's direction. "I don't mean to sound callous, but that issue sold very, very well. Nelda was a looker, and she had a legion of country music fans."

"She also had a son," Darcy recalled, "who threatened to sue us for publishing the article."

Elaine dismissed that. "Not a leg to stand on. I put Legal on alert and never heard another word. We printed what she told us, most of it verbatim."

"What do you know about the son?" Marlowe asked.

He was perched on the windowsill, in faded jeans and a green T-shirt. With his hair messy and with two days' worth of stubble on his face, he looked scrumptious—a fact, Darcy noticed, that wasn't lost on her editor.

Lips pursed, Elaine tapped her glasses to her throat. "Rumor has it he's been in rehab nine or ten times. He's probably about thirty. I'm not sure, but I think there might be some other problems. Nelda mentioned having to deal with blockhead child psychiatrists as one of the reasons she turned to meds."

"I found the article," Darcy said from her desk. "And a photo of her, but there's nothing on her son."

"Police might have a file." Marlowe hopped down. "Where does he live?"

"He threatened to file charges through a lawyer in Memphis," Darcy recalled. "He might be there."

Still tapping her glasses, Elaine made a circuit of the office. "I see a wealth of possibilities developing here. Promise me this story's ours when it's resolved, Darcy. Or, hell, now for that matter."

"No story now." Val came in, looking pale and wearing sunglasses.

Elaine raised a brow. "Cop?"

"Yes." Darcy smiled a little at her skeptical expression. "There's nothing else here, Marlowe. Even our Tennessee affiliate doesn't mention a son. I'll copy the relevant articles, but I have a feeling he stayed, or Nelda kept him, in the background as much as possible."

Val pushed on his left temple. "Darcy, you recognized two other names on Lugo's private list, right? I didn't just dream that."

"Yes, they were—"

"On the list," Marlowe inserted smoothly.

He didn't have to look at Elaine. Darcy could see the avid gleam in her editor's eyes from across the room. Quickly copying the necessary files, she slipped the disk into her purse.

"Are we done here?" Marlowe asked.

"Say yes." Val worked his jaw to loosen it. "I'm in serious need of caffeine."

"I can help you with that, Detective." Elaine pulled out her BlackBerry. "I have a great little deli on call. They're a twenty-four-hour deal, and they deliver. Come to my office, and you'll be swimming in coffee before you know it."

That wasn't all he'd be doing if Elaine had her way. It wouldn't help. Val didn't know the other names, and hungover or not, Darcy suspected he was too smart to fall for her tricks. Still, Elaine was nothing if not hopeful.

Marlowe nodded toward the door. Shutting down, Darcy collected her bags.

She was a step ahead of him when she heard the crash on the other side of the wall—followed by a woman's short, sharp scream.

"Grogan needs serious help." Hunched over a table in the deli Elaine had mentioned, Val gently kneaded his eyelids. "I'll grant you, taking a cell cam into the women's washroom and hiding out in one of the stalls is messed up. But getting caught while trying to sneak a peek up the skirt of a woman who's old enough to be his grandmother, that's sick."

Marlowe watched for Darcy at the entrance. "The Peeping Tom thing was an afterthought, Val, a bonus from his perspective. The building's being rewired. He was using a cutout on his side of the wall to listen in on our conversation."

"Doesn't make him any less sick." When the coffee arrived, Val pounced on it. "Keep it coming," he told the server.

Over his cup, Marlowe saw Darcy approach the table. "How did you get in?"

"Kitchen entrance." She lifted her hair so the wall fan could cool the skin on the back of her neck. "The owner likes me."

Not a hard thing to do, he reflected.

Kicking back, he let the tension go and enjoyed the view. "What's happening at the magazine?"

"All hell's still breaking loose, but while Elaine's assistant might want to press charges right now, she probably won't. Means there'll be something extra in her Christmas envelope."

"Sick," Val repeated.

"Take heart, Detective, there was some payback involved. Her scream startled Trace so badly, he banged into the wall and gave himself a black eye."

Val polished off his coffee, exhaled loudly. "Back to business. What was that dead singer's name?"

"Nelda Hickey."

"Okay, we search for information on the son. And the other names you recognized?"

"Wilkie and Lyons," Darcy replied. "You might recognize R.J. Wilkie's name. He anchored the news hour for a local cable station."

"Doesn't ring any bells. Did you know him?"

"Met him. Asked if I could interview him. Never heard from him again. He went on vacation and just dropped out of sight."

"Dropped out as in missing person?" Marlowe asked.

"I honestly don't know."

"Why did you want an interview?"

"Human interest, mostly. I'm not all about scandal and exposure. Sometimes warm and fuzzy's a pleasant counterpoint. R.J. appeared to fit the bill."

"What's the story with Lyons?" Marlowe asked.

"No story, I just recognize the name."

"From?"

"Other media sources, the occasional high-profile fundraiser. LyonsCorp is an amalgam of maybe ten heavy-duty tool companies, acquired over the lifespan of its founder, Constantine Lyons, who'd be in his mid-nineties by now. Constantine's one and only son gave him three grandchildren, all boys, all now in their thirties. The oldest races cars, primarily in the Southeast. One of the others—I'm not sure which—was arrested for possession of an illegal weapon. I think he might have gotten into drugs, as well. But of course, Granddad hushed it up."

"And corporate headquarters are?"

"In Los Angeles."

"Like the Macos."

"Like them, yes, but grandson's rumored drug problem aside, there was no connection between the families that I ever heard of."

Marlowe picked up a menu, but didn't read it. "Are you sure those are the only names you know?"

"I went over the list five times, Marlowe. I have an excellent memory for names and faces. I'm sure. I'm also late for an appointment. Make mine to go, Randy," she called to the counterman.

He gave her a wink and two thumbs-up.

Marlowe's eyes narrowed. "Exactly how well do you know that guy, Darcy?"

Late or not, she took a moment to lean in and show him just enough cleavage to kindle a fire in his lower body. "Well, let's see. We had dinner together last month, once at his place, once at mine. He broiled a really succulent leg of lamb." She made a slow circle on his forearm with her finger. It wasn't until he glanced up that he saw the tease dancing in her eyes. "Gotcha again. I know him because I work out at the gym three times a week." She moved closer to whisper, "With his wife."

Marlowe's gaze fastened on hers for several long seconds.

She didn't look away, and truthfully, he didn't know where it would have gone from there if Val hadn't cleared his throat and scraped his chair across the tiles. "I'll take my coffee to another corner, shall I?"

Darcy smiled, held her position for another steamy second, then backed off. "No need, Val. I really do have an appointment." She widened her eyes at Marlowe's stare. "With my doctor. I travel, remember? I'm overdue for a series of booster shots." Sliding her purse strap over her shoulder, she stood. "I still think this is Vince Maco's deal. None of the people on Lugo's private list have a reason to want me dead. Frankie's is the only life I've affected in a direct and negative way. The Macos make sense. Right down to the guy in the Yankees baseball cap. Vince hired him to kill Lugo once Lugo's usefulness ended. Now it's on to me."

Marlowe kept his tone neutral. "I didn't see Maco's name on Lugo's list, Darcy."

"You can't be sure that's the only list he had. You're being a mule, Marlowe." But her eyes were still dancing when she fisted his hair and gave him a hot, hard kiss.

She was gone before his vision cleared. Val was beaming and the counterman was staring longingly at the door.

Crowd noises buzzed in his head. Dishes clinked, fans whirred. Then reality hit. His cell rang.

"Still 'Tears in Heaven'?" Val gave his head a shake. "It's time to move on, M."

Ignoring the remark, Marlowe unhooked his phone, glanced at the screen before answering. "What's up?"

Clearly feeling better, Val sang to himself as he drummed his knuckles restlessly.

"Yeah, I'll tell him. You're sure about Maco?"

The singing stopped. "Who is that?" Val asked. "What about Maco?"

Marlowe held up a hand, listened for another few seconds, then ended the call. "Frankie's had two strokes in the past month."

"And the other question?"

"It was no one, Val. A contact."

"His name wouldn't be Blydon, would it?"

Sitting back, Marlowe rehooked his phone. "Okay, yes, it was Blydon."

"Why's he calling you? I have a cell, too, you know."

"And it's where?"

"Right— Uh, hell." Val closed a bloodshot eye. "On my dash."

"That's what Blydon said."

"Great. What else did he say?"

"That Frankie's not expected to make it."

"Third stroke's usually a killer. The business reins'll be in son Vince's hands. If Darcy's right about the Macos and sonny boy's smart, maybe he'll call off his hit man once Papa's gone."

"Maybe we can find out."

"How? Fly to L.A.?" Val considered the idea. "Actually, I could handle that."

"So could I, but it's not gonna happen."

"Oh, come on. One mistake and Captain Bligh sticks me back behind a desk?"

Grinning, Marlowe raised his mug. "Nothing that drastic, old friend. Vince isn't in California." His eyes glittered. "He's in Atlantic City."

Chapter Eight

Darcy arrived at her doctor's office with five minutes to spare. She got her shots and then detoured to historic Elfreth's Alley for a chat with a woman who would be celebrating her one-hundred-and-sixth birthday in late September.

Between the woman's refusal to wear a hearing aid and Darcy's concern that the baseball cap guy might have followed her to the interview, their conversation had an off-kilter feel to it. Like the tilt of the centuries-old floor.

Darcy cut the morning short and returned to the office.

Not surprisingly, Elaine was still fuming about the incident with Trace and her assistant. On the positive side, Darcy was able to slip in unnoticed and spend some time with her computer.

At the end of three frustrating hours, she found herself wanting to punch something—preferably with Maco's face on it.

Or maybe she'd find Marlowe instead, push him down and tear off his clothes. Yeah, that could work. She was in the mood to bite hard right now.

"Darcy?"

She was also in the mood to snap. However, for the sake of workplace harmony, she summoned a pleasant tone.

"I'm busy, Trace. Go away."

Of course, he didn't. Shoulders stiff, he came to stand in front of her desk. "I'm not a pervert."

She glanced up. "Good to know. Bye."

He didn't move. "Hickey's son lived in Los Angeles until last year. Now, he's in New York."

Darcy regarded him with a blend of suspicion and curiosity. "Are you sure?"

"Would I say it if I wasn't?"

Would he? Standing, she walked to the water cooler and drew herself a glass. "Go on."

"He does impersonations."

She stopped the glass halfway to her mouth. "Of who?"

"Different celebrities. It's a sort of jumbled musical montage. The trouble is, he tends to go through it at warp speed."

"Right. Does he also go through rehab?"

"Every few months."

"Drugs or alcohol?"

"Mostly cocaine, I think."

Which was, or had been, Frankie Maco's primary source of income.

Darcy's smile had a lethal edge.

Using the fingers of her right hand, coupled with that smile, Darcy nudged Trace toward her sofa. "Why don't you sit down right there. One call, and we'll have a nice long talk. About a man who could potentially be a murderer. And how you happen to have so much information on him."

"YOU SPENT TWO HOURS in your office with a guy who looks up old women's skirts?" When Darcy didn't stop walking, Marlowe caught her arm. "Are you nuts?"

She swatted at his hand. "It's been suggested. Let go of me, Marlowe, or at least keep moving. Hospitals freak me out. And for what in this case? All I got from Matilda was a vague reference to a pair of blue shoes and a compliment on my blond hair."

"She has a bullet wound and a concussion, Darcy." He slowed her down, but didn't stop her as she made for the exit. "She'll be more coherent in a day or two."

"Which could be good or bad, depending on how you view it."

"You're wondering why she was attacked at the shelter, aren't you?"

"Aren't you? Matilda saw the killer. She can identify him. He has to locate and eliminate her. But he messes up, then he compounds his mistake by running from the scene. He hops in a cab. Driver sees him, too. Yet that man's alive and unharmed. Why?"

"Opportunity," Marlowe said simply. "The killer couldn't get to the cabdriver through his cage. And if he'd shot him at the drop-off point, a hundred people would have seen him. The plan's falling apart from his perspective. Time to reevaluate. Things aren't going smoothly. Okay, he tried to take out a homeless woman. But the cops are watching the driver. Pursuing that problem's too risky. He has to let the guy go, focus, do the job he was hired to do."

Darcy refused to laugh. "Well, I feel better."

"This will end," Marlowe promised, still holding her arm. "In the meantime, be glad no one who shouldn't be dead is."

"Oh, I'm glad about that—although I'm not sure Lugo would think he deserves to be dead." She paused. "What do you think Matilda meant about blue shoes?"

"Maybe the guy was wearing blue sneakers."

"Maybe. Anyway, the fact that she noticed my hair proves her vision's fine, so that's a plus."

She twisted on her arm. "Did I mention that hospitals freak me out?"

Had he mentioned that he liked her hair, too? And every other damn thing about her?

"Think of this as a nightmare winding down," he suggested, but let her pick up the pace. "We've placed Vince Maco in Atlantic City and Nelda Hickey's son at the Boho…"

"Boka," she corrected. "The Boka Club in lower Manhattan. Trace says he does everything from Buddy Holly to Eminem, with a hefty dose of Cher mixed in. Unfortunately, I couldn't get a straight answer from him about how he knows that. I called Elaine in to help pump him, but no luck." She broke off as they emerged through a side exit. "It's still light. I thought it must be past midnight by now."

"Not even close. But the light you see is strictly ahead of us. Behind is all black cloud."

She lifted her face to the sky in search of a breeze. "If there's a thunderstorm attached to those clouds, I hope it's packing a strong wind. The air's gone dead—no foreshadowing intended."

Marlowe searched his jean pockets for keys. "You spent too long with your boss's cousin today. He sucked the optimism out of you."

"No, I was good until we hit the hospital." She

raised her left arm. "I fractured my wrist when I was in Jakarta with my mother. She was on leave and wanted to do a little trekking. I thought a summer vacation sounded like fun, but I quickly learned that some countries have very low standards of health care."

"Scarred you for life, huh?"

"This life and the next three, none of which I'm eager to move on to, so backtrack to the singer's son. Are the police checking him out?"

Marlowe kept an eye on the lights flickering inside the clouds as he unlocked the passenger door. "Val left for New York when we left for the hospital. I figured you'd rather do Atlantic City."

Delighted, she grabbed his face and gave him one hell of a kiss on the mouth. "Casanova couldn't hold a candle."

His thoughts scattered as heat speared from his lungs straight to his groin. "Uh, why?"

She kissed him again with gusto. "You knew what I'd want. You cared."

Kudos to him, he reflected. They'd been talking about Atlantic City, right?

When she hooked her arms over his shoulders, he wondered if she realized she was blowing his system apart cell by screaming cell.

"Darcy…"

"Yes, I know. The time and place are not

good." She tugged on the ends of his hair. "When do we leave?"

Trapping her jaw between his thumb and fingers, he feathered his lips across hers. "Tomorrow," he said, and let the sparks zinging through his veins ignite a fire he hadn't experienced in years. "I have a different plan for tonight."

FORTY MINUTES LATER, they were standing inside a cramped pantry at the boardinghouse. Overhead, deep rumbles of thunder made the jars and bottles clink, while the smell of dried herbs threatened to make Darcy sneeze.

Marlowe's plan wasn't exactly what she'd envisioned. But it was an intriguing idea—planting a fake garrote in the kitchen. And they were together, so the good outweighed the bad. Who knew, she might even live long enough to tell her grandchildren the sordid details.

With her cheek pressed against Marlowe's neck, she strained to see through the cracked door. "Anything?" she whispered.

"We've only been here for five minutes, Darcy."

"So claustrophobia's not a problem for you."

"I have my moments."

His murmured response made her laugh. She tickled his shoulder. "I love it when you go all cryptic on me. Are you sure anyone coming into the kitchen will see it?"

He cast her a dry look. "Maybe not, but as traps go, I thought it might be too obvious to hang it from the pot rack."

"And so we segue from cryptic to moody." But she stopped talking when they heard footsteps in the hallway.

Cristian poked his head around the swinging door. "Aunt Hannah? Are you here?"

The way his face brightened when he realized she wasn't had a laugh climbing into Darcy's throat. He looked like a kid whose teacher hadn't showed up for class.

Shedding his pack, he came inside. He paused when he spotted the garrote, cocked his head this way and that, then picked it up and twirled it like a jump rope.

"Cool," he said, but brought his brows together. "Kind of weird though, Auntie."

Setting it on the island, he went to the fridge, rooted around for a minute and then finally maneuvered his carefully balanced plates across the floor and back through the door.

"Well, that was dull." As more thunder rattled the shelves, Darcy leaned against one of the posts and let her eyes travel around the shadowy pantry. Not surprisingly, they came to rest on Marlowe.

She battled a sigh. How long could a normal, healthy female be expected to ignore such an incredibly hot male? He smelled like soap and sex and man, and if she hadn't been keeping the words *time* and *place* firmly in mind, she probably would have pushed him a lot harder by now.

Because she appeared to be the only one affected by the tight quarters, Darcy kicked his ankle.

He looked back. "What?"

"Nothing. Just moving my foot." She heard a swish behind her. "Great, now the cat squeezes in."

Marlowe crouched. "Is this the cat I've seen in your yard?"

"His name's Hodgepodge."

"Yours?"

"No, but I feed him. Money for pets tends to be a bit tight around here."

"Why?"

"Hannah's husband gambles it on sports."

"So I've heard."

He stopped as the kitchen door squeaked open and a second person entered.

When Marlowe remained in his crouch, Darcy went to her knees behind him. "Who is it?"

"Hancock." Marlowe's hand moved to the gun

at the back of his jeans. "And he's not a happy man."

Not happy at all, Darcy acknowledged. Hancock snatched the garrote from the counter so fast she almost missed the motion. What she didn't miss were his bared teeth. Or the fact that his darting eyes came to rest on the pantry door.

"Up," Marlowe said, and drew her to the far wall.

Podge stretched, front paws first, followed by the back ones.

And meowed.

Darcy's heart slammed into her ribs. Through the slit on the hinged side, she watched Hancock wind the cord around his hands and snap it.

"What's he doing?" Marlowe asked in her ear.

"Coming this way. And he's angry."

Thunder shook the jars again. Podge pawed at the door. On impulse, Darcy used her foot to ease it open just far enough for the cat to amble out.

Uncertainty slowed the man's advance. "Was it only you in there, cat?"

Podge stared for a moment, then flattened his ears and hissed. Hancock immediately stopped snapping.

Voices in the hall brought him around. His features tightened. Giving the cat a wide berth, he stuffed the garrote down the front of his pants and hastened toward the rear staircase seconds before Hannah and her husband pushed through the swinging door.

DARCY TOOK MARLOWE TO a crowded Greek restaurant, where the lights were low, the noise level was high and the platters were stacked with food. Colorful dancers worked the limited space between tables. Smoke and shadows hung like a thick veil in the heavily spiced air.

"I can't believe a murderer would try anything here," Darcy shouted above the music. She made an elaborate hand gesture at one of the servers and was immediately waved to the back wall.

"Another gym pal?" Marlowe surmised.

"We do yoga together from time to time. Her uncle owns this restaurant and two others in the city."

A woman bumped her on one side, a man on the other.

"I'm not sure this is any safer than a walk in the park." Marlowe took her hand and, Darcy suspected, a hard jab to the ribs. "Is that the table she meant?"

"It's reserved for family. If unoccupied, yoga pals qualify."

Grateful to have made it, Darcy sank onto the padded bench. "Now that we're semisafe in a crowd, let's talk about Mr. Hancock. He took the garrote. Obviously he recognized it. Does that mean he's the one who left it in my closet? Possibly. Unless someone stole it from him to use on me. Unlikely. Did Mrs. B. know it was there? I want to say no, but money talks, and I gather from the discussion she and her hubby had tonight that he lost some number of thousands when the Phillies fell to the Rangers on Monday. Brings us full circle to the so-called root of all evil."

Marlowe picked up the ouzo that had magically appeared in front of him. "You think Hannah Brewster has it in her to strangle you?"

"What, you don't think a woman's capable? My mother can take down a guy with fifty pounds on her. It's called technique, and it's not as uncommon as you might think."

"Having been taken down by a female instructor at the police academy, I won't argue. However, from what I've seen, Hannah's not into technique."

"No, she's into snooping. It's possible she spotted Hancock heading for my place and followed him. He realized what was happening, hid, then took off, minus his weapon, when she wasn't looking. I realize believing that would mean there are two people after me, which sucks, but it isn't completely unreasonable where the Macos are concerned."

Marlowe poked at a heaped platter, which, like the drink, had simply materialized in front of them. "Does everyone here get the same dinner, or did I make an unconscious hand motion, and this is the result?"

Darcy gave him a napkin. "I made the motion. My friend's uncle is hearing impaired. I know a little sign language. She knows a lot."

He shook his head. "I'm never going to fully understand you, am I?"

"Probably not. Doesn't mean we can't have hot sex. At some point," she added when his eyes slid to hers. "After we polish off this mountain of souvlaki."

When he still didn't say anything, she smiled and glanced away. Then she paused as her gaze returned to the seat. To a brown envelope that was stuffed in the side pocket of her purse.

"Uh, Marlowe?"

"What, you want a doggy bag?"

She continued to stare. "There's an envelope in my bag."

"And that's significant because?"

"It didn't come in here with me."

HE WATCHED THEM FROM across the room. Tuning out the boisterous Greek music, he let a more soothing song play in his head. Elvis hadn't been totally rockabilly in those early years. He'd done a ballad or two, as well.

Ballads soothed him almost as much as the P.I. pissed him off. He honed in, crooned with The King and waited for her reaction.

It was starting to hinge on reaction. That and keeping the anger in line.

The envelope came out, the flap went up, the contents emerged.

He licked his lips and savored the moment.

He could see she didn't like it. Neither did the P.I., but he hardly mattered. The message was for her. Sent, received and unreturnable.

The ballad oozed through his head like molasses. Sweet and oh so lovely.

He drew the moment out, salivated through it. Soon he'd taste it. Soon her life here would be his to control.

And a brand-new era would begin.

Chapter Nine

"He removed you from the picture, Marlowe." In the passenger seat of his Land Rover, Darcy traced an *X* in the air. "He slashed your face with a red pen. Three of those slashes cut through the photo paper. That says fury to me. And fury says Vince Maco."

"You're really stuck on him, aren't you?" Using the heel of his hand, Marlowe gave the AC control a thump. "If the Macos are angry because Frankie's dying and, thanks to you, his final years were spent in prison, why eliminate only me from a picture the killer obviously took of us together in the park?"

"As a warning."

"Of what? Death? Seems redundant at this point."

She sighed. "Fine, you explain it. I'm too tired to theorize. What little sleep I got last night was riddled with nightmares."

"About Frankie and company?"

"Partly." Crossing her legs, she tugged on the hem of her dress. "The last ones involved the past." She uncapped a bottle of juice, drank. "I got a few threats when I worked in northern California."

He stopped abusing the panel. "What kind of threats?"

"Indirect ones. Our news team was accosted on location a few times by a logger with a grudge. But he was shouting at his employer more than us. We just reported what was already an ugly truth within the company."

"Anything else?"

"There's always feedback," she said after a moment. "Some positive, some not. Some. personal, some not. A musician wrote me once and told me I inspired him visually. He said he wrote his lyrics while he watched my newscasts."

"And the not-positive stuff?"

"Come on, Marlowe, it's the nature of the work. You slant a newscast one way, people on the other side object. I learned early on not to take criticism personally. It's also a big stretch from criticism to death threats. Anyway, there was more positive feedback than negative. And many, many kind gestures."

"For example?"

"I got flowers from someone called Lover Boy."

"Excuse me?"

She smiled sweetly. "Everyone who saw the handwriting on the card put his age upward of eighty."

"Was that ever verified?"

"Well, no, since I had no reason to be paranoid in those days."

"Did people ever send pictures?"

"Sometimes. Of themselves, their pets, new babies, that sort of thing. One viewer sent a shot of me holding a rescued puppy. Another had me walking through a hotel lobby in Los Angeles. It was cool because the background was blurred, so it looked like I was moving out of time."

"What were the circumstances?"

"I was covering a senatorial election race."

"Was there a note with the photo?"

"No." She sent him a canny look as the air-conditioning finally kicked in. "But there was a heart drawn around my head."

"Do you still have the picture?"

"I'm not sure. Marlowe, nothing happened. These weren't unique or isolated incidents. One of the women I worked with in Los Angeles had a stalker after her. Now that was cause for concern. Notes, pictures, flowers, sometimes even jewelry used to appear in the office. Once, the guy actually called to tell her how much he loved her. She was out, so I took the call. He went all soft and creepy, thinking I was her. He said one day they'd be together forever."

"Did the police make an arrest?"

A faint frown marred her brow. "I don't remember. Probably. In any case, the gifts stopped coming. Six months later, she left the newspaper. I had the office to myself, and my byline space was expanded. All things moving forward in S.L. Hunt's world."

"Until she met Frankie Maco."

Leaning toward the windshield, Darcy let her gaze sweep the twilight skyline of Atlantic City. "It was a good situation for a while. Unfortunately for Frankie, S.L. met a man who gave her the means to write a series of articles that focused a little too much attention on the family business. Being a career-driven woman, S.L. saw media gold in that information. She collected and collated, and in the end handed her gold mine over to the authorities. Because, above all else, she'd been raised to be a good American citizen."

Marlowe's eyes went first to her legs, then to her face. "Are you sure you don't have any of those letters or photographs?"

"Not sure at all, so, yes, I'll go through my boxes. I still have stuff on Frankie. Maybe I've forgotten or overlooked some detail of the trial."

"What was Frankie's lawyer's name?"

"Kasparidian, Ezekiel J. The press called him Jabba the Hutt. Is that relevant?"

"Means you probably haven't overlooked any details." With the boardwalk in sight, Marlowe pulled over.

"Look, why don't we—" she began. Then forgot the question when he took her face between his fingers.

Less than half a second later, his mouth crushed down on hers in a kiss that sent every rational thought spiraling into oblivion.

Heat and color fused. A hundred other sensations flooded in. They swam in her head even after he drew away.

"Okay," she said shakily. "What was that for?"

"My own satisfaction." He slid a knuckle over her cheek. "My pleasure. I've been staring at your legs since we left Philadelphia. Something had to give."

"I'd be flattered if I didn't sense a but."

"We're in Atlantic City, Darcy. It's time for positive action." His eyes glittered as they looked into hers. "Let's see if we can't hook a California shark."

"TWENTY-THREE BLACK. The lady wins again."

Despite the lucky drop, Darcy glanced behind

her. The icy finger that trailed down her spine for the third time in five minutes no longer set her teeth on edge, but it made her want to move.

"Not liking this," she decided as she gathered her chips and left the roulette table. "Time for you to reappear, Marlowe."

When he didn't right away, she studied the faces around her. Nobody appeared to be watching. She hadn't seen a man in a Yankees cap and she hadn't spotted Vince Maco.

She did spot Marlowe several yards ahead as he returned from the men's room.

Black pants, white shirt, black jacket slung over his right shoulder, the man was a sin waiting to happen. Half the women in the casino would probably love to inhale him in one long, sensuous breath. Darcy certainly would.

Or not, she thought as another chill skidded down her back.

"Have you seen Vince?" she asked when Marlowe joined her. "Or the baseball-cap guy?"

"Not yet. You?"

"No, but I've been having a Big Brother feeling since I scored my first win at the roulette wheel."

A faint smile appeared as Marlowe's gaze traveled around the noisy floor. "You won more than once?"

"Twice. It's my limit at any gaming table."

Resolved not to let unpleasantness win, she knocked his arm with hers. "Guess that means dinner's on me, huh?"

"We'll see. I talked to Val while I was in the washroom. Nelda Hickey's son was at the Boka Club until last Sunday. That's when his short-term contract expired. The club's Web site still lists him as the feature performer, so Val says he'll stay on it for another night. The guy might turn up." He frowned when her eyes fastened on a point over his shoulder. "Something?"

"I saw a Yankees cap at the casino entrance. It's gone now."

"Lots of people wear baseball caps, Darcy." But she noticed he scanned the entrance.

Using the color, lights and music as a balm, Darcy regrouped. "I talked to a man at the roulette wheel while you were gone. He says the owner here is looking for investors. He thinks he's heard the name Maco through the grapevine."

At the arch of Marlowe's brow, she sighed.

"Not every business in Frankie's sphere is crooked. He bought a legitimate and quite respectable chain of hardware stores a year before he was indicted. As far as I know, it's still in the family. Not that that probably matters to you, since you appear to be leaning in a different direction."

"There's such a thing as duplicity, Darcy. Whoever's after you could be using Frankie Maco's threats to cover his or her actions."

Where was a drink when you needed one? she thought. "You want me to go into hiding, don't you?"

"It's an idea."

"It was an idea three years ago. I agreed, and where am I now? Back in the starting blocks. You can buy time if you're lucky, Marlowe, but you can never be sure. Yes, that's true of life in general, and God knows, I'm an advocate of change, but I don't like doing it at the end of a shotgun." Because he was so teasable and she was so tired of tension, she angled her body toward him. "I might, however, be persuaded to hide out for a single night."

The head-to-toe look he gave her seared her skin.

"Maybe I'll rephrase that." She hooked a finger in the opening of his shirt. "We only made one booking for the night, and I'm going to guess the room service here is excellent."

She took another step, then shivered as the eerie sensation returned full force. "Okay, that's it. Someone's watching me. If it isn't the baseball-cap guy, it must be Vince. Do you see anyone looking this way?"

"Yeah, about ten men and that's only in the immediate vicinity." Marlowe ran his thumb over her collarbone. "You don't exactly blend into a crowd, Darcy."

"Thank you, but I still feel something."

Taking her hand, Marlowe linked her fingers with his. "About that booking," he began, but got no further as a man three feet away from them shouted, "Wait a minute, you! Stop!"

The woman he shoved aside stumbled between Marlowe and Darcy. She would have fallen if Marlowe hadn't caught her.

Using his arms like machetes, the man hacked his way through the crowd. "He stole my wallet!" he shouted. "The one in the blue shirt!"

"Are you all right?" Darcy asked the woman he'd shoved.

"I saw him do it." The elderly female patted her thin chest. "It wasn't the man in the blue shirt. The thief was wearing brown. The man in blue was just walking past. He ran, so maybe he was in on it, but the one in the brown cowboy shirt is the thief."

"Blond hair, ponytail?" Marlowe handed his jacket to Darcy.

"Yes, that's him... Oh, goodness, my heart." The woman sighed. "This trip was meant to be a birthday gift from the Red Hat Society. I'm eighty-seven tomorrow."

"Marlowe." Darcy grabbed his forearm. "Let Security handle this."

"Security's following the blue man. Ponytail's heading for the lobby."

He was gone before she could object.

The old woman continued to pat her heart. "I hope the thief doesn't have a knife. Your young man could get hurt."

"You'll never convince him of that." Darcy watched Marlowe until she couldn't see him anymore, then turned back. "Do you want to sit down?"

"If it's not too much trouble. My friends went up to their rooms an hour ago." She flapped an arthritic wrist. "The corridor behind the slot machines is quiet and comfortable. I'll be able to catch my breath."

Darcy kept watch for Marlowe as they crossed the casino. Once, when the skin on her neck prickled, she tossed a frustrated look over her shoulder.

"I'm not imagining this," she stated, and got the woman looking with her.

"Did you spot another thief? Oh, good, we're here."

Darcy's instincts screamed at her not to go into a deserted corridor. There was no one to be seen in either direction, and a secondary commotion had broken out near the lobby entrance. However, with the woman sagging against her, she had no choice but to swap instinct for need and let the door close behind them.

A strange hush descended. Her companion welcomed it. Darcy's nerves went on alert.

The old woman pulled a cell phone from her purse. "I'll call Charlie, my fiancé, in Newark, and fill him in on the news. He's such a worry-wart. Can you get him for me, dear?"

Darcy dialed, watched the door. At least the corridor was well lit, and there was a second exit in plain sight.

She needed a gym, Darcy decided, handing over the phone. The headache that lurked at the base of her skull begged for motion. Something involving Marlowe would be good. But anything away from this empty corridor would work right now.

"Say good-night to Charlie," she urged the woman in a murmur. She walked, rubbed her arms, turned…

And saw the door begin to open.

She had her keys out and palmed when a bow-legged man in faded denim lurched across the threshold. A larger man with a firm grip on his arm followed.

Darcy swallowed a shaky laugh. All that adrenaline for nothing more sinister than a drunk and a bouncer. Maybe she should consider going into hiding after all.

The bouncer handed the drunk to an even larger man behind him.

"Problem, miss?" he inquired as his charge was ushered outside.

Slipping her keys back into her purse, Darcy explained. Minutes later, the old woman was rolling toward the elevator in a sleek leather chair.

"You have a nice time with your young man," she called around the bouncer's arm.

"Wish he was," Darcy murmured.

Rolling her head, she turned—or started to.

Halfway around, a man's hand clamped over her mouth. As his arm cinched her waist, his voice—thick, syrupy and sporting a familiar, though not-quite-right twang—flowed into her ear.

"Nighty-night, pretty darling. We're caught in a trap for the moment, but we'll get ourselves out soon enough."

Darcy's vision wobbled. He'd used a cloth to cover her nose and mouth. And she knew, she just knew, she'd inhaled some of the chloroform on it.

Words jumbled. The lights around her blurred. She heard voices, a woman laughing. Then everything swirled together. And slowly faded to black.

Chapter Ten

Marlowe swore all the way back to the casino. He'd spotted the guy in the Yankees cap. He'd have been able to nail him if he hadn't had the casino thief pinned against a wall and two dozen excited bystanders endeavoring to help.

The man knew he'd been seen. Before Marlowe could hand the thief off, the guy had bolted.

His cell rang as he wove a path through the sea of confusion that was currently the casino lobby.

"What's with the racket?" Val shouted. "I thought you'd have swung a romantic interlude with your fair lady by now."

Marlowe squeezed past a clump of tipsy Texans and wished he could stop the world for sixty seconds while he located and removed Darcy from the madness.

What did he care about thieves, or addictions, or people tossing away their hard-earned cash?

He'd be stripping off Darcy's pretty strapless dress. Though he might leave the spiky red stilettos. With her blond hair and big blue eyes, she'd be a total siren.

"You there?"

Marlowe made one last sweep of the lobby. "Yeah, I'm here. Do you have something?"

"What I have is a sore finger from punching numbers all day and night. Here's the scoop, old friend… I got in touch with the Boka Club's manager. He said young Hickey took his vocal act on the road at the end of last week. It's a twisty one that winds across the eastern states and hits all the major cities, from New York to Virginia Beach. Top of the list, our very own Philadelphia, Pa."

DARCY WOKE UP—or, more precisely, surfaced—from a lifeless black void to the more familiar environs of a hotel room.

Furniture took shape as her bleary eyes adjusted.

She allowed herself ten precious seconds, breathed carefully, tried not to wonder how she'd gotten here, only how she could get away.

Her head felt heavy when she moved it. And she swore someone had shoved a knife into her left temple.

But she knew instinctively there was no time for pain. She had to get past it, find a way out.

Going up on her elbows, she listened. Music played somewhere close by. Beneath it, she heard the murmur of a man's voice.

Distorted memories swam in her head. Faces without features and the smell of alcohol blended with perfume, laughter. Flamingo-pink finger-nails.

The voice droned on, became a sonorous buzz in the background. She couldn't see the speaker or anyone as she worked her way from the sofa. All the rooms in the hotel were suites. He must be in the bedroom.

The door doubled up in front of her. Closing her eyes, she concentrated, brought the space dimly into focus.

Her heels sank into the thick pile carpet. Good. No telltale sound to give her away. Unless he heard her heart banging in her chest or the blood pounding in her ears.

The door handle came into view. She twisted, pulled, prayed.

The voice halted. Her breath hitched. She yanked the door open, made it to the corridor.

Different music played out here. Ignoring the fact that her limbs weighed three hundred pounds, she zeroed in on the stairwell. Did she hear him shouting behind her, or was her mind amplifying fear?

Palms damp, she pushed on the fire door. Frigid air poured over her shoulders and arms. She shivered, but caught the metal rail with both hands and started down.

The stairs went on forever. So did the shadows. They clung to the high corners, gave her heart yet another reason to race. As if she needed that with her head on the verge of exploding.

To keep herself balanced, she counted. Panic wanted in, but she shoved it back. Deal with the now, react later, she told herself.

Or not, she thought as a loud clunk reached her from above.

Okay, now she had to react.

She spied the red exit sign. Careful not to catch a heel, she ran for it and shoved on the bar.

It barely budged.

Feet slapping the treads above seemed to be gaining speed.

"Open," she hissed, and shoved again.

This time the door flew back. Because she'd expected it to stick, momentum threw her across the threshold.

Straight into a black wall.

WHERE THE HELL HAD she gone? Marlowe was out of places to look.

He'd tried their suite, the casino and all the corridors surrounding it. He'd gone through a

legion of hotel shops, six lounges and seven restaurants. And turned up nothing. A floor-by-floor
search was all that remained.

Enlisting the help of two security guards who'd
seen her earlier, Marlowe expanded his perimeters.

Sirens blasted through the terror that wanted to
swamp him. He heard a shot, out of time and
way out of step with the situation.

Faces circled, overlapped. Some were hazy,
others were more clearly defined. Darcy's was
the most clearly defined of all.

One corridor bled into another. Until…

Far ahead, a guard waved an arm.

"Got something here, Marlowe."

Four people stood, leaned and swayed around
him. Three of them wore lopsided smiles. The
fourth lounged against the wall, eyes closed,
mouth open.

"These people saw a blonde woman who
looked like Ms. Nolan behind the casino." The
guard winced as the lone female stepped on his
foot. "They said she was with someone."

"It was a man," the woman confided in a loud
whisper that reeked of alcohol.

"Tell me about the blonde woman," Marlowe
demanded.

"Nice hooters," one of the men piped up.
"Killer legs."

"Killer shoes." The woman toppled into Marlowe's chest.

He took her by the arms. "Did you see who she was with? The man? What did he look like?"

"Not sure. Think he was wearing a hat. Red. Or, no, that was the shoes."

Marlowe shook her to keep her on track. "Was he tall, short, heavy, thin?"

"Not fat," she said, then frowned. "Don't think. No, not fat. Maybe brown hair."

"Blonde." The man with the closed eyes chortled. "Man, she was a looker. Face of an angel, but, whoo hoo, more than a tad tipsy. Guy wound up carrying her."

"Where?" Marlowe asked.

"Elevator."

"Wouldn't let us on," another man put in. "Jerk got there after we did, barged in and closed the door... And his hair was black, like the hat." He cocked a thumb at his chest, missed and jabbed the underside of his chin. "Black hat, black hair, red shoes. That's him."

The last man, shorter than Marlowe by six inches, crept in low to peer up at his face. "You, uh, mind letting go of my woman there, dude?"

Marlowe removed his hands. "Look, all I want is my own woman back." And one clear shot at the bastard who'd taken her.

"It was the hat that made his hair black." Pushing the short man away, the woman leaned back into Marlowe. "I like dark hair, so I'd have noticed if he'd had it. Like I noticed her shoes."

"Try seven," one of the others suggested. "Think maybe the elevator stopped there."

"Or that's as high as he can count after eight shots of whiskey," the smaller man added.

Marlowe moved aside, spoke to the guards behind him. "Let's go with seven."

It was only two flights up, less than ten seconds away by elevator. But every one of those seconds read like an hour in Marlowe's mind.

When they exited on the seventh floor, one of the guards went left. The second, who'd come with him, rolled his eyes as they rounded a corner. "Man, what a night. Drunks everywhere."

This particular drunk was cursing as he attempted to pull a fire door open.

"Swings away from you," the guard called, and gave it a shove.

Marlowe snagged the drunk's jacket to keep him from falling, then did a quick double take as Darcy tumbled across the threshold into his chest.

Her knee came up automatically. Unprepared, Marlowe took the full force of the blow.

Pain burst outward from his groin. His face went pale and his limbs turned to rubber, but he didn't slacken his grip, and his eyes never lost their focus.

"Darcy, stop. It's me."

Her fist only plowed halfway into his stomach before her head shot up.

"Marlowe?" Her startled exclamation ended on a long release of breath. She dropped her head to his throat. "Thank God. I thought he'd gotten ahead of me."

Gripping her arms, he pulled her upright, searched her eyes. "Are you hurt? Did he hit you, cut you, anything?"

"No… No." Focused urgency returned, and she swung her head around. "There's someone behind me. I think it might be him."

One of the security men squeezed past. "I'm on it. Up?"

"Fourteen," Darcy told him. "Room number's 1472."

Marlowe brushed the hair from her cheeks while she struggled with a memory.

"I didn't see him, or anything really. I think he was on the phone. I heard a voice, but it sounded weird, like Charlie Brown's teacher. No distinguishable words."

"And you're sure you're not hurt?"

"I'm fine. He used chloroform, same as at my place. I stopped breathing right away, so I didn't inhale as much as he thought I did. Still, I got enough that I knew I was going to pass out. There were people, though, I remember that. Voices—talking, laughing. Pink nail polish."

Marlowe let his forehead fall into hers. "I talked to the people you saw, Darcy. Their descriptions of the man holding you varied widely. The woman was blinded by your shoes. The men appreciated…other things."

"They thought I was drunk, didn't they?"

"Face of an angel, soul of a sot."

A sigh escaped her. "I'd have probably thought the same thing myself." Her gaze returned to the stairwell. "I could have sworn he was behind me. It must have been someone else…" She trailed off, gnawed on her lip. "I felt him when he grabbed me, Marlowe. He had the same build as the guy at my place. Whippy muscles. Really strong. That's not it, though. When I woke up…" She curled her fingers into his shirt, concentrated. "Something about an angel."

"What, like a picture?"

"No, like what you just said. Face of an angel. Or maybe it was a devil." She hummed a tune he almost recognized. The third time through, recognition struck. "That's it!" she exclaimed. "The music! It was different in the room than in the hall outside. He was playing 'Devil in Disguise.'" Her gaze snapped back to his. "He was playing Elvis."

NIGHT SLOWLY MELTED INTO day. No surprise to Darcy, a search of the stairwell came up empty. So did the suite where she'd woken up. No one could remember who'd reserved it under the name Darcy Shannon or prepaid for its use in cash. The best the desk clerk could offer was that it had been a "regular kind of guy."

So much for the power of observation.

With her glam sunglasses securely in place and skinny silver shoes replacing the red ones from the previous evening, Darcy used the heat and sunlight on the boardwalk to exorcise the last of her headache. That plus four extra-strength aspirins.

She hated to think how many painkillers Marlowe must have needed to offset the damage she'd inflicted with her knee.

They'd spent most of the morning at police headquarters. The hotel room had been dusted for fingerprints and scoured for clues. Nothing had come of it so far, and Darcy didn't expect much would. The bathroom hadn't been used, the bed hadn't been touched, the minifridge remained fully stocked.

"And so, heads down and racing, we slam into

yet another brick wall." She glanced at Marlowe as they walked. "So far this trip, we're coming up empty. I haven't even seen Vince Maco yet, and he's the main reason we're here."

"Which either means he doesn't know you're here because he's not behind the attacks, or, if he is behind them, he's smart enough to distance himself."

"Opt for the second, unless you like the hands-on suggestion I put forward at breakfast."

"That Maco's doing his own dirty work?" Darcy was glad to hear Marlowe chuckle. "I think you can relegate that one to the bottom of the list."

"I don't know. You said you saw the baseball-cap guy after you caught the thief in the hotel lobby. You also said he ran out of the building."

"What, he couldn't have reentered through another door?"

"Reentered, located and drugged me, switched his cap for a hat, then whisked me up to a room he'd reserved under the name Darcy Shannon?"

"The name's irrelevant, and the time frame's tight but workable." Marlowe lifted his sunglasses to regard her. "In any case, we don't know that Baseball Cap's a solo act. He probably has backup."

"Courtesy of Vince Maco, who, I promise you, would have made a point of being in that suite when I woke up."

"Uh-huh. So you think it was Vince you heard in the bedroom."

"Could have been."

"Describe him to me."

"Tall, dark, long arms, broad shoulders—a bit like the baseball-cap guy, actually. Enough like him that without seeing his face, I still say it could have been Vince who grabbed me. Except—" she made a wafting motion "—there was no cologne."

"Is that significant?"

"No, just a point. Vince was in love with cologne three years ago." She shrugged. "Maybe his tastes have changed. Whatever the case, Vince's last words to me were 'Someone, someday. Anyone, any day. With me being the most likely anyone of all.' End quote."

"You're not going to open your mind here at all, are you?"

"If I can avoid it, no."

But really, she reflected, was there such a vast difference between Vince wanting her dead and someone else wanting the same thing? Just because Vince Maco might prefer to kill her personally, that didn't mean he would. For all she knew, the man in the plaid shorts walking five feet in front of her could be on the Maco payroll.

And wasn't that a cheerful thought?

She swept up Marlowe's hand and gave it a playful pull. "To hell with death, hit men and Vince Maco. I've gone over what happened so many times, I can't see it clearly anymore. So—" her eyes began to dance "—as long as we're nearby, and before the horror crashes back in, I'd like at least one Ferris wheel ride out of this trip."

Of all the responses he could have made, every muscle in his body going tense wasn't the one Darcy expected. Ferris wheels were fun things. Weren't they?

Unsure, she touched his arm. "Marlowe? Are you all right?"

She could tell he forced the tension down. Didn't lose it, but took it to a manageable place.

"Yeah, I'm good." A faint smile hovered on his profile. "Some people have skeletons, I have a ghost. Life's all about deflecting our demons."

Darcy nodded, but said nothing. When someone mattered—and she was beginning to realize he did—she could lock her curiosity away and toss the key.

"Look, if you're hungry we can go…" She stopped, stared, then drew back, palms raised. "Okay, that's it. I'm officially freaked."

Marlowe frowned. "What's wrong?"

"Look left. There's a man playing hide-and-seek behind one of those bronze columns. Unless I'm seeing things, that poorly hidden man is Trace Grogan."

Chapter Eleven

The sun was a big orange ball by the time Marlowe let her coworker escape. Even from a distance, Darcy was impressed. The man might not be a cop these days, but he could still bring the goods to the table. Or to the boardwalk, in this case.

Caught red-handed, red-faced, Trace hadn't put up much of a fight. He'd spluttered for thirty minutes. He'd denied for another ten. Then finally, left with no out, he'd caved.

He'd admitted to following Darcy from Philadelphia. His mission? To obtain a story with which to placate his cousin and boss.

"Word's out that some part of my past has caught up to my present," Darcy told Marlowe as they continued to walk along the boardwalk. "Ding, ding, light goes on in Trace's head. Discover what that something is and maybe he can avoid a pink slip." She offered him some of her popcorn. "On the other hand, maybe he's lying."

Marlowe smiled. "You think?"

"Well, he could be on the Maco payroll. His current job's in jeopardy, so I can see him selling out."

"How would he know who to sell out to?"

"News flash, ace. He's not above eavesdropping. Anytime, anywhere, even outside my house if he thought it would be worth his while."

"We'll see."

Darcy watched him sift through the dwindling crowd on the pier. He disliked amusement parks; she got that part. What she couldn't figure out, and was still resolved not to ask, was why.

Something to do with the mysterious Lisa perhaps? He'd spoken of a ghost. Maybe there was a fatality involved.

Dropping the popcorn bag in a trash bin, Darcy hooked his arm and steered him away from the rides. It surprised her that he resisted.

"I thought you wanted to ride the Ferris wheel."

"I do, but you don't. I'm trying to be nice. We can play the slots instead, have a quiet, candlelight dinner and, barring disaster, see what develops from there. No pickpockets, no chloroform and, for what it's worth, no Elvis."

"That's called a clue, Darcy, a potentially solid lead."

"Oh, good. So we'll just round up all the Elvis fans currently staying in Atlantic City and see what jumps out at us, shall we? Maybe R.J. Wilkie, vanishing news anchor extraordinaire, decided to ditch his life in order to become an Elvis impersonator. Or Constantine Lyons is living out one last fantasy before he dies. Even Vince could have a thing for The King. And let's not forget our most likely candidate, Nelda Hickey's Tennessee-born son, although that accent sounded off to me. He makes his living mimicking singers."

Marlowe smiled ever so slightly, then unhooked and ran his hands over her arms. Bringing her slowly onto her toes, he gave her a kiss that, for all its brevity, sent an arrow of need from her mouth straight to her belly.

"Wow." She made a cascading motion with her fingers. "Think I'm seeing stars. You're an incredible kisser, Marlowe… Uh, was I talking before you did that?"

"Yeah. You were trying to distract me. While I appreciate the effort, I have to face my demons sometime, and tonight works as well for me as tomorrow."

She could have pressed, was truly dying to know, but she smiled instead and dropped her sunglasses back in place. "Okay. If you insist."

Marlowe eyed the oversized wheel that rose several stories into the twilight sky. "This should be interesting."

His cell phone rang as they were settling into the cage.

Darcy looked around the pier while he talked and let the jumble of puzzle pieces in her head fall where they chose.

Not that there were many to fall. The hotel and casino surveillance cameras hadn't revealed much. Whoever the guy was, he knew how to work a security system. If he'd gone into the casino, no one could pick him out of the crowd. And he must have altered the view of the corridor cam, because all the disks revealed was a great deal of wall and carpet.

Okay, maybe they'd gotten a shot of the guy's feet. It hadn't helped.

As for the elevator cam, the consensus was that he'd draped a napkin over the lens before it had captured him.

Planning and execution, Darcy reflected. This

guy had sized the situation up, played the odds and won.

Until she'd regained consciousness.

The wheel bumped up, then stopped to let more riders on. Lifting her face briefly to the early-evening sky, Darcy tuned back in to Marlowe's conversation. Except there wasn't any because he'd just ended it.

She slanted him a circumspect look. "Was that a good or bad call?"

"One of the security guards at the hotel is sending a picture of Vince Maco."

"Do I want to see?" she asked when the cell phone beeped.

"Your call." But he handed the cell phone over and left it to her to decide.

"Why do I know this is going to be— Oh my God!" Disbelief fostered near shock. "Is that Vince?" She shook the phone as if to alter reality. When nothing changed, she used the zoom to bring him closer.

Setting an arm across her shoulders, Marlowe grinned. "Doesn't look quite the same as his DMV shot, does he?"

For the life of her, Darcy didn't know what to say. The man who'd grabbed her both last night and outside her home had been agile, one hundred and eighty pounds at best.

Unlike Vince Maco, whose current weight almost certainly topped three hundred.

"YOU'RE A COP."

They were the first words out of Vince's mouth. He scowled a little but didn't look overly worried. Waving the hotel staff away, he settled back in the Cove Lounge with his hands folded over his more than ample belly.

"If this is about my Uncle Remo's trip to South America last week, he's visiting a lady friend. You should know that. You've got people following him from one side of Buenos Aires to—"

"It's about Umer Lugo."

"Who?" Vince's thick brows came together. "Is he a cop, too?"

"He's a lawyer," Marlowe said. "A dead one."

"Well, my sympathies to his family. Am I supposed to know him?"

"It's been suggested."

"So's the Second Coming. Hasn't happened yet that I'm aware of. Do you like steak?"

"Not as much as I like answers."

Vince spread sausagelike fingers. "I've got nothing to hide these days. My old man's had two strokes. He knows he won't be around much longer. Maybe he's known for a while. He put me in charge of his business concerns more than eighteen months ago, told me to clean things up for him so when his time came, he could meet St. Peter with a clear conscience."

Marlowe masked a grin. "You don't think he's aiming a bit high, all things considered?"

"Shoot for the stars, who knows what happens. Point your gun the other way, you might shoot off your foot. I've never heard of that guy you said."

"Umer Lugo."

"Sounds like he should be making vampire movies. And before you start with the blood money cracks, I'll tell you straight out, I've been doing what my father asked. You might not think gambling's clean, but it's a hell of a distance from where my family used to be. Now, let's get down to brass tacks here." He used his hands to demonstrate. "Do you like your steak two inches thick and rare? Or over-done and flat like the soles of my grandma's orthopedic shoes?"

UPSTAIRS IN THE SUMPTUOUS suite Marlowe had snagged for them, Darcy ran a warm, peach-scented bath.

Every room in the hotel had windows. The long bank before her showcased the moon, the stars and the ocean shoreline. The water was serene at the moment, but Darcy knew those same waves would be raging by October.

Which pretty much described her own current state of mind. Calm on the surface, wild and crashing inside.

Thanks to Marlowe's activated cell phone, she hadn't missed a single word of his conversation with Vince Maco. And after several glasses of expensive brandy, he'd said quite a bit. About his father, his family, his past, his present and his future.

Did she believe him? Jury was still out, but she had to admit she was leaning.

"Damn you, Vince," she said on a sigh.

Outside, the night sky sparkled. While the tub filled behind her, Darcy identified five constellations. She didn't want to think about any of it. Most especially she didn't want to think about Marlowe.

The man was dark and dangerous, a fascinating puzzle best left unsolved. Her life was complicated enough. She didn't need love sneaking in and turning complicated to crazy.

Thoughts pitched and whirled in her head. Raising a finger, she used the tiny points of starlight to draw a waterfall in the air. Then she watched her thoughts wash away, like a stream of false beliefs slipping into oblivion.

Shutting off the water, she opted for a few extra minutes with the night.

What could you do when everything you thought was true turned out to be an illusion? "Poof." She made a starburst with her fingers. "All gone. The Reaper's still behind you, Darcy, but now you have no idea who sent him."

"You're getting closer day by day. Doesn't that count?" Marlowe's voice came from the doorway.

Darcy merely smiled and sipped the wine she'd poured earlier. "Want some?" She dangled the glass in his general direction. "Bordeaux and steak works for most of us."

She felt him behind her as he took the glass. "What can I say? The man knows his red meat."

"Oh, Vince knows lots of things. Most of them used to be bad."

"Does that mean you believe him?"

She wondered if it was a touch of hysteria that made her want to laugh. Or scream. She went with the laugh and swung on her heel to face him.

"You have no idea how badly I want to say no, Marlowe. I mean, come on, the guy's a practiced liar. He also thought you were a cop—a misconception I notice you didn't correct—so, who knows, the lies might have been automatic. But I could tell that you believed him, so I poured a glass of wine and toasted the man. The man whose apparently empty threats single-handedly tore my life off one path and slammed it onto the one you see today. Do I resent that? Surprisingly, I don't. Why?" She fingered his shirt. "Because there are so many worse places I could be than standing in a spa bathroom in a luxury hotel in Atlantic City with a superhot man less than two feet away from me."

A slow smile curved her lips, as venting gave way to desire. "So I ask myself, what might that man be thinking right now? That I'm insane? Maybe. Or is it possible he's thinking there are many worse places he could be as well?"

Darcy spied the glitter in his eyes. Undisguised and, she hoped this once, uncontrolled.

Expectation spiked. Sex with this man wouldn't be soft and sweet. It would be a wild ride into an unknown world.

She caught his waistband with her fingers, but didn't tug. Instead, she eased closer, let her eyes slide down, then up again with a seductive twinkle. "Many worse places, Marlowe," she repeated. "But not many better."

"Not any better."

It was the first time she'd heard it. The unbridled desire. The hunger. The barely leashed restraint she'd sensed in kisses that had taken him to the edge, but never allowed him to tumble.

There were times, she decided, when self-control needed a good sucker punch.

His gaze steady, Marlowe ran his hands up and under the sleeves of her robe. Dark rose silk, like the flush that swept across her skin. His gaze skimmed her body beneath the delicate fabric. The light in his eyes deepened as he inclined his head.

Darcy glimpsed a predatory expression on his amazing features. A second later, she lost both the vision and her train of thought.

His mouth on hers was pure fire, greed fueling hunger, hunger spawning a much deeper need.

Her hands explored the sleek muscles of his shoulders and back. Everything about him reminded her of a panther, right down to the murky darkness that seemed to dwell in his soul.

The needful curl in her stomach spread through her body. He made a sound in his throat that brought a deep shiver. Something feral and instinctive, like an animal.

Were they moving? Darcy thought they might be. Or did the sensation of floating come from the twist of colored light outside the windows?

Her hands went to work on the snap of his pants. Heat radiated from him.

She gave a muffled cry when his mouth found her breast. Her head fell back, her breath emerged as a shocked gasp.

When her heart pounded, she welcomed it, used it, savored the strong, hard beat and every other sensation that rocked her.

Her feverish fingers tugged at his shirt, worked it off. The ends of his hair skimmed her neck. Hungry for more, she pulled and yanked and probably tore.

Her robe fluttered to the floor. Her feet left the solid surface as her legs locked around his hips.

Skin to skin, Marlowe laid her against the downy duvet, burning her flesh from head to toe.

Her mind whipped and whirled. Her belly quivered. He was all flesh and bone and long, supple muscle. When his mouth returned to feed on hers, she breathed into him and cupped his face.

She didn't want to sample, she wanted to taste. To know. To drink in the complex flavors of the man.

He rolled her under him and she felt the full force of his erection. Sensation erupted, so intense it brought a surge of white heat to her throat and abdomen. Need speared downward between her legs and made her breath hitch. Her fingernails bit into his back. Her hips bucked.

"Whoa," he said softly in her ear. "I want this to last. For both of us."

Now, there was an intriguing thought. Through the myriad sensations clashing wildly inside her, amusement reared its head.

Grabbing two fistfuls of hair, Darcy held fast, not to keep him close, but to hold him away, just enough so their lips no longer touched.

"So near and yet so far." She moved her head, didn't quite graze his mouth. "Is this what you want, Marlowe? The pain of self-denial?"

A hint of a smile appeared. In spite of her stranglehold on his hair, he kissed her. "Yeah, this is it. I love the pain. I love all of it."

Lowering his head, he set his lips on the hollow spot at the base of her throat. "It's early, Darcy, as nights go. We've got a lot of hours left."

Relaxing her grip, she nuzzled his cheek. "Aren't you the patient one all of a sudden."

"Not patient," he corrected, still with that faint smile. "Just in tune with my body." In the shimmering wash of light, his eyes caught and held hers. "With my soul."

The sparkle gentled. Maybe sweet had its merits after all.

To her delight, it also had its limits, even for

Marlowe. When his mouth took possession of hers again, gentle quickly gave way to savage, restraint to urgency.

Her body assumed a life of its own. She let her neck arch and sensation rule as wave after pleasured wave poured through her, sweeping the world and all its problems away.

He moved against her in that lovely sexual rhythm she'd somehow known would beat between them. He cuffed her wrists briefly on either side of her head, then released and laced his fingers through hers.

She bit the lobe of his ear, skimmed her teeth along his jaw, nipped his lower lip. He answered by using his tongue, delving into the deepest regions of her mouth and robbing her of breath.

At the sound in her throat, he lifted his head, smiled and brought his body up over hers.

Even by the faint light of the stars through the bedroom window, Darcy couldn't miss the gleam in his eyes. Invigorated, she freed and lowered her hands, then closed her fingers around him. She drew him deep, deep inside.

Need and hunger collided. Sparks snapped to flame. Everything shifted, everything turned hazy, inside and out.

Darcy's hips came up. Her legs tightened and held. She rode him as he plunged into her. Once, twice, again and again. With every thrust, her heart slammed against her ribs.

More, was all she thought. More and more and more.

It stunned her that she could feel so much without feeling any one thing at all. If the whole was better than the sum of its parts, this had to be the universe, this truly staggering climax like nothing she'd imagined and even now only half believed. It tossed her up in an eruption of fire and swept her seamlessly over the peak.

Where had this come from? she wondered distantly. This passion. Had it been living inside her all her life, and was she only realizing it now, with Marlowe?

The question died, simply faded away like a single dark cloud in a sky gone soft and luminous.

Time stopped, or seemed to. Until…

With her body limp and her mind still dazed, Darcy became aware of Marlowe lying on top of her. Or more correctly, collapsed on top of her.

She didn't know if it was his heart or hers that thundered against her breast. She only knew she couldn't move, couldn't swallow, could barely breathe.

Was this shell shock? The aftermath of an explosion too powerful to deal with? Might be closer to implosion in her case, but whatever it was, the leftover force rocked her almost as strongly as it had when she'd been trapped in the center of it.

Her hands lay on either side of her head, fingers curled. A form of surrender? The notion brought a smile—which was good, because it proved at least some of her muscles worked.

She continued to float, to savor. Life just didn't get any better than this. Body to body, with Marlowe inside her and the danger far, far away.

The physical danger, anyway.

"Go away," she directed the stray thought and, closing her eyes, concentrated on the moment.

"If you're talking to me, use my voice mail." Marlowe spoke facedown into her hair. "I'm incommunicado for the next week."

"I don't think the hotel will let us keep the room that long." Darcy kissed his hair, smiled as she stroked the ends. "Pretty sure I heard something about a medical convention."

"Might come in handy if we try that again."

"Only if we wind up dead. It's a convention of forensic pathologists. But, hey, no harm in trying. Whoa!" She laughed when he grabbed her. "What are you doing?"

The laugh became a gasp as he rolled them both over. Suddenly she was on top of him, her hands on his shoulders, her legs straddling his hips.

"I wanted a better view," he said with a grin.

Darcy let her palms slide along his ribs. She leaned forward, until her mouth was less than an inch from his. "I believe I like it up here, Mr. P.I. Makes me feel very powerful."

"Really? It's making me hard."

"Hard and fast. As always, I'm impressed. Fair warning, though. I have extremely high standards." She sank her teeth lightly into his bottom lip. "By morning, I expect to be completely blown away."

Chapter Twelve

Marlowe didn't know if he'd met her expectations or not, but she sure as hell had met his. Exceeded and shattered them, in fact.

As dawn crept over the horizon, he rolled onto his back and stared at the shifting shadows on the ceiling.

A glass of wine would be good, but he didn't need it as much as he needed a clear head, so he'd settle for a shot of caffeine and a wicked new memory.

Darcy had rocked him last night. She'd swept his barriers aside as if they were air. Then she'd wrapped herself around him, body and soul, until all he could see, all he could think about, taste and feel was her.

She was incredible, with her sleek curves, her soft skin and her silky hair. She was heat and color and light. She was fire and she was steel.

She was more than his messed-up brain could

deal with right now. So he'd deal later, he decided, and, moving carefully, got out of bed.

Asleep on her stomach, she looked like an angel, with her head turned on the pillow and her fingers curled loosely on the sheet. An angel with a kick.

Unbidden, a song played in his memory as he headed for the bathroom. Whoever had taken her from outside the casino had been playing Elvis, he remembered. Might be a clue. Might not.

Ditto Umer Lugo's private client list. Darcy had recognized three names. It didn't necessarily follow that any of those people wanted her dead. It only meant she knew their names.

Could the killer still be Vince Maco or someone connected to him?

Marlowe's cop sense said no. But his instincts weren't infallible. It wouldn't hurt to concentrate on several different areas. If he could ever concentrate again after last night.

The bath Darcy had run was cold, the bubbles long since popped. As he turned on the water in the marble shower, Marlowe wondered if his own bubble would do the same thing before this was over. Did he want it to pop, or, God help him, did he want to start something entirely different in his life?

Swearing softly, he turned the hot water up higher. He'd felt the burn inside too many times to count last night. Now he wanted it on his skin.

He was in the shower and soaping his shoulders when he spied her through the glass door. Leaning against the vanity, she had her arms folded loosely across her robe-covered chest and one bare foot hooked over the other.

"There are better ways to exorcise demons or erase memories than by searing off a layer of skin, Marlowe. Last night was incredible, but as I've said before, not a lifetime commitment."

He stopped scrubbing to brace his hands on the wall in front of him and send her a faintly ironic sideways look. "I agree, it was phenomenal. But it's not a fear of commitment I'm trying to sear off. It's fear, plain and simple."

Pushing upright, she let her robe fall open— and instantly sent his pulse rate through the roof.

"Would that fear involve me, yourself or everything that's happened?"

His laugh had a rough edge. "Take your pick, Darcy. They all work." He looked away. "There are a lot of things you don't know about me, about my life, my past."

Now it was her turn to laugh. "Oh, Marlowe, I could say exactly the same thing to you. You're not alone, and I'm not easily shocked. Or put off. Or undone."

She started toward him, into the hot spray. "As for last night, I have to say I was a bit shocked. I was also completely undone. But nothing about you has put me off to this point, so why would you think anything could?"

Letting her robe drop, she slid a seductive finger along his side, from ribs to buttocks.

"Which brings us full circle to those secrets we both appear to have. Guess maybe we should deal with some of them, huh?"

"Yeah, we could do that." His voice came out so grainy, he barely recognized it. Shoving off, he turned the water temperature down and with his other hand, drew her into the full, warm spray. "Or we could do this instead."

And with his eyes locked on her face, he slowly lowered his mouth to hers.

THIS WASN'T ACCEPTABLE!

The P.I. could help her the way a P.I. was supposed to, but touching her wasn't allowed.

She belonged to him. Okay, she didn't know it yet because maybe he hadn't made himself clear in the beginning. But crossing the P.I. out of the picture he'd given her should have made some kind of statement. Like, hello, Darcy, send the guy packing before he gets crossed out for real.

Which had almost happened once already and definitely would again.

His chest heaved as one ugly thought after another streaked through his head. Feeling the rage, he pressed his fists to his temples.

Control, he reminded himself. Don't be angry. Put on the false face. Wear it, work it, make them believe. Then…pow!

He played the music in his head…

No, no, it's not healthy to obsess. Don't fixate. The King's good. He's great…

Don't get stuck on him. Don't stick on anything. On anyone.

The woman's beautiful. She's perfect…

Never use that word! Bad word! Bad concept!

Man, it was hard to please some people. Okay, she's flawless. Better?

The music played on. Soon "Heartbreak Hotel" would fade away. Tricky job, though, to hit on the final song. Something that mirrored what Darcy was now.

Flawless.

Something that spoke of what Darcy would soon be.

Dead.

DARCY SPENT HER FIRST morning back at work feeling very, very good, a little feline and completely rejuvenated.

Atlantic City had been a revelation. Not so

much in the beginning, but in the end a delightful detour from her day-to-day life.

Making love with Marlowe had stunned her. It had truly been an eye-opening experience. The question was, did she want her eyes open, or would it be wiser all around if she simply closed them again, and with them her heart?

Because he'd touched something inside her. And once touched, it would be difficult to backtrack. It might be impossible.

One thing was certain—the heat and humidity in Philadelphia hadn't diminished in her absence. Neither had the frenetic pace at the magazine.

Elaine ambushed her as she returned from lunch. "I need the piece on Congressman Budder."

At Darcy's abstract response, a hand came out to snag her arm. "What was that? Fobbing me off's not an answer." She gave a firm yank. "At your most preoccupied, you don't fob. So now I'm doubly curious. What happened in Atlantic City?"

Darcy smiled. "It had its moments. Some of them were spectacular. Others I could have lived without." Pushing through her office door, she took a look around and stopped dead still.

"Someone's been here."

"Yes, you, all morning," said Elaine from behind her.

"I went out for lunch. That's thirty minutes of me not here."

"You and everyone else on this level. Except me."

Darcy circled her desk. Something about the configuration on top felt wrong. "Where was Trace?" she asked.

"In the art department all morning. I've spoken to him three times in the past hour, and God knows how many times over the past few days."

"Oh? He calls you when he's off the clock?"

"He's brownnosing, darling, trying to scoop some story about a mobster, I think. Yes, I know, he can't string two sentences together, but a scoop's a scoop. Besides, he's afraid I'll can him if my assistant quits." Pivoting, she trailed Darcy into the adjoining office and back. "What is it that has you peering into every nook and cranny of this office?"

"My stapler's been moved."

"Excuse me?"

"Don't give me that look. I admit it's anal, but my stapler always sits next to my out-box, never my in-box."

"That's not anal, kiddo, that's borderline OCD."

"I'm not obsessive or compulsive. I'm organized. Keyboard's wrong, too," she noted thoughtfully.

"Maybe someone from downstairs came in looking for something. You weren't here, so he or she did a quick paw-through before he or she left."

"Maybe." Moving the mouse, Darcy started to open a drawer. But the picture that materialized on the computer monitor froze her fingers. "Better make that maybe a no."

"What? Why?" Elaine scooted around the side. "Has someone…?" She leaned forward, adjusted her glasses. "What is that?"

Darcy didn't need to get closer. The image was frighteningly clear.

"It's a headstone, Elaine. A grave marker." Her gaze fixed on the gruesome granite face, and more specifically on the five words carved there in bold, black letters. Simple, chilling words that read:

IN MEMORY OF
SHANNON HUNT

"I KNOW, I KNOW. I'm twenty minutes late, and Captain Bligh's on the warpath." Val groped his way into the detectives' room. "No lectures. My head'll blow at the first cross word."

Marlowe directed a faint grin into the file he was scanning. "You're in luck, Detective Reade.

Blydon's tearing one of your lieutenants apart for screwing up an unwarranted search."

"There, you see? I'm not the only one who gets it wrong." Leaving his sunglasses in place, Val took a tentative sip of his take-out coffee. "What's that you're reading, and should I know about it?"

"I accessed more files from the disk I down-loaded in Lugo's motel room. Nothing that connects so far, but you might see something I'm missing."

"Doubt it." Val drank, raised his glasses, winced. "Man, that's bright." He dropped them back down. "How was Atlantic City? In a non-professional capacity, that is. I already know about the abduction part."

Marlowe made one last scan of the file. "None of your business." He picked up his own coffee. "I ran into a brunette in Records. She asked me if you were back from your Jersey Shore weekend yet."

His friend frowned. "Why'd she ask you about me?"

"Saw us together, I imagine." A brow went up. "Jersey Shore, Val?"

"New York, New Jersey, she got it wrong is all. She's hell on wheels on a computer, not so strong on memory." He moved a shoulder, changed the subject. "I put out feelers for Nelda Hickey's son. If he's got a gig in this city, he's playing it under another name. Makes my job a thousand times harder, but I'll stay on it."

"He's into smack, right? Do you have anyone who knows the street suppliers?"

"Two. Not sure how reliable they are. You?"

"I might know someone." Marlowe's gaze traveled to the window, but returned when he heard a wolf whistle and glimpsed blond hair.

With a quick smile for the suspect in cuffs who'd emitted it, Darcy sidestepped a blood-smeared female and two detectives who suddenly looked a lot less bored with life.

She had that effect, Marlowe conceded. Earlier tonight, when he'd been thinking about Ferris wheels, he'd brought Darcy to mind before the usual screams and sirens.

Burying that, he stood from the corner of Val's desk. Her body language and facial expression were at odds, and not in a good way.

With Val on his heels, he started across the room. "What is it?" He couldn't see any marks, nothing to indicate she'd been in a struggle.

She handed him a sheet of paper. "This was on my computer when I got back from lunch."

Marlowe's stomach muscles clenched as he

read the words, but he schooled his features and kept his expression neutral.

Val took the opposite tack, yanking off his sunglasses and staring red-eyed at the printout. "Well, hell, that's not good."

Marlowe glanced at her. "E-mail?"

"No, someone set up a file and left it for me to find." At his speculative look, she spread her fingers. "I don't know if it was Trace or not. It's possible. He's at the magazine today. But if it was him, he's gone from calculated risk taker to moron in a very short time. Elaine's all over him about this, so much so that I didn't have the heart to tell her about our encounter in Atlantic City."

"What encounter?" Val asked, looking a bit perkier.

"Grogan showed up." Marlowe reread the words. "Did you touch the keypad?"

"No, but it won't matter," she said. "Whoever did this more than likely wore gloves."

"We'll dust for prints anyway." Val pressed on a nerve in his neck. "I'll take a patrol over right now, question the staff."

"It was lunchtime," she told him. "Picture rats on a sinking ship. Anyone who hangs around risks having Elaine drop extra chores on their already overburdened shoulders." She tapped Marlowe's forearm with a contemplative fingernail. "Come to think of it, though, Trace didn't go out for lunch. Not that that's unusual, because as we all know, he loves to lurk."

Val snorted. "I'll make a point of having a chat with him."

"With what's left of him," Darcy corrected. "Elaine's not feeling merciful. And since I'm bound to be next on her interrogation list, I'm in no hurry to get back. It says Shannon Hunt on the headstone," she reminded Val. "I go by Darcy Nolan. Not that it makes much difference at this point. She's been suspicious for a while."

Marlowe studied the printout, noted two black lines running across the bottom of the grave marker.

While Val braved his captain's office, Marlowe perched again on the desk and, bringing Darcy to his side, showed her the paper. "You're twenty-twenty. Are those words?"

Turning the printout this way and that, she finally shook her head. "I think they're ink smears."

"In case they aren't, let's take a quick drive by your office."

"You're not thinking that's a signature, are you? I mean, whoever this guy is, and insane though he might be, he's not wacko enough to sign his name."

"All things being equal, I agree." Marlowe gave her a hard kiss before taking her hand and standing. "But things might not be equal anymore."

"Which means?"

"It's possible he wants you to know who he is."

OF ALL THE THINGS MARLOWE could have said, a homicidal nutcase wanting her to know his identity was hardly the most encouraging.

However, from a psychological standpoint, it made sense.

Several aborted murder attempts later, frustration must be setting in. She should be dead. All should have been revealed. Satisfaction should rule.

Instead, she'd evaded death and escaped. A happy ending from her perspective, somewhat less fulfilling from his.

"I feel like I'm foundering without Vince and Frankie to pin this on." Darcy used her ID card at the rear entrance of the building. "It's me," she called to a passing guard.

He gave her a thumbs-up and vanished. At Marlowe's amused look, she poked his stomach.

"Yes, former lieutenant, I sneak in the back way from time to time. You're not here to judge. This is about smudges and headstones and who besides the Macos might know about Shannon."

"Grogan has access to a mountain of information."

"None of which would connect Shannon to Darcy. But I say again, Trace isn't above eavesdropping, so, yes, he could know the truth." She snared his arm and turned right. "We'll take the service elevator. It opens one short corridor from my office." She noticed his smile as they entered the car. "That's an intriguing expression you have on your gorgeous face. Are you wondering if I found out after some wild office Christmas party?"

"No, I'm wondering if you ever went out with Vince Maco."

"Ah, well." Unprepared for that, she pushed the button.

"Yes, or no?"

"No. I had dinner with him once, but…"

"Sounds like a yes to me."

Sounded like irritation to her. Fortunately, patience was one of her stronger points. "It's a no, Marlowe. Vince knew I wanted a story. He asked me out. I assumed he meant out where I could interview him. But being Vince and having an ego the size of a Boeing 747, substitute the word *intimate* for *interview.* He took me to his uncle's upscale Malibu restaurant."

"Tito Garcia's?"

"That's the one. I didn't want to make a scene, so I went with it."

"Then used your wiles on him."

"You make me sound like Eve shoving an apple in Adam's mouth. I got him talking."

"And drunk?"

She stepped out of the elevator into the corridor. "You're not inspiring me to finish this story."

"Okay, Vince talked." Marlowe's dark brow went up. "And then?"

"Nothing. He'd been too well trained by Frankie to let anything slip. We finished our meal, and we left."

"That's it?"

Darcy ignored the doubt in his tone. "That's it," she said. But then she thought it through and sighed. "Almost. He called me again. And again. He said I affected him like no other woman ever had. Personally, I think he just hated being refused." With a quick sideways glance, she crossed to her office door. "It took a while, but he got the message."

"Are you sure?"

"Of course I am. Where did this even come from?"

He turned her toward the desk. "I'll let you know after we enhance the picture."

"Marlowe, Vince isn't in love with me. He never was. He simply doesn't like the word *no*."

"Uh-huh." Already working, Marlowe enlarged the image once, and again. "Come here, Darcy." He pulled her down next to him. "Tell me what you see."

"A very big headstone with a very creepy message on it."

"Go lower."

She honed in, could almost make something out of what had initially appeared to be two squiggly lines. "Can you enlarge it any more?"

He zoomed in on the area and was able to focus on the smudges.

Except they weren't smudges anymore. They were words—reedy, miniature, and terrifying.

Darcy wanted to jerk away, but morbid fascination kept her riveted as the words glared up at her.

THE TRUTH IS CARVED IN
STONE

She reread the lines three times. Each time, she felt the knots in her stomach grow tighter.

"Stone." Staring at her, Marlowe said the last thing she wanted to hear. "You used that surname when you did the weather in Oregon, right?"

The knots tightened. "You have an excellent memory. Now tell me what you think it means—

beyond the obvious fact that whoever left this and knows I was Shannon Hunt also appears to know I was Shannon Stone."

Marlowe worked the image, pulling the entire marker back into the frame. "It either means someone's done his homework on you or…"

"What? He's playing games with my head before he kills me? Wonderful. Mission accomplished."

"You're reacting, Darcy, not looking."

"Of course I'm reacting." But she looked again. "Shannon Hunt, Shannon Stone…" Then, as if a giant hand had wrapped itself around her vocal cords, she trailed off. "Oh, hell." She traced the barely visible line with her eyes. "That's carved right into the headstone, isn't it?"

"I'd say."

A feather tipped with ice skimmed along her spine as she finally recognized the line that ran up, down and around the marker for what it was.

A heart.

Chapter Thirteen

Obsession…

Is that what was fuelling this nightmare? Not a grudge, but someone who'd seen her on the West Coast and had possibly stalked her there? Someone who, with Umer Lugo's help, had tracked her to Philadelphia?

Darcy had done enough stories on the subject to understand the MO. Obsessed individual stalks object of desire. Stalking leads to eventual disillusionment, disillusionment to death.

Apparently the person after her had reached the fatal fourth stage.

Three and a half hours at the police station didn't clarify a thing. By 7:00 p.m. her head was muddier than ever and her nerves were tight enough to snap.

It helped a little when Val suggested the three of them brainstorm over appetizers at a South Philly club. It didn't help that a pitcher of beer materialized on the table thirty seconds after they arrived.

"Interesting crowd." Darcy set her chin on the back of her linked fingers and looked around. "Do you make a habit of mingling with the criminal element? I've seen money and small packages change hands three times, and we've only been here a minute."

"I'm hoping to meet an informant," Val told her. "That's a lot of what this place is about. Look on the bright side, Darcy. Being in a den of thieves will keep your mind off the bigger picture."

"Yes, I'll let you know how that works out. Where's Marlowe?"

"I saw him following someone into the alley." He picked up the pitcher. "Only the best on tap."

"Keep the criminal customer satisfied, huh?"

"Cop customers, too. I count ten in the vicinity."

"So I should feel really safe here."

"Well, they're mostly undercover, hooking up with sources, playing a role. Stakes are often high. You can't count on too much support."

"And the fear comes crashing back in."

Val poured a full mug, but to her relief drank sparingly. "Talk to me about your past, Darcy. Guys you might have brushed off without realizing it."

"Val, if I didn't realize it, I can't tell you about them, can I?"

"Nelda Hickey's son."

"Never met him."

"You saw the picture I found."

"But he was in full Ozzy Osbourne makeup."

"Good point. Constantine Lyons?"

"Again, never met him. Or his son, or his grandsons."

"Three grandsons."

"The oldest races cars. The second's had some legal problems. The third—no idea."

"Marlowe came up with a few things while you were talking to Blydon."

"Wonderful. Tell me number three's an obsessed killer, and we're set."

"That'd be too easy. Truth is, young Lyons works for Granddad's corporation. Ditto troubled middle brother, whose legal problems range from numerous DUIs to smashing up a couple of Grandpa's Jags."

"I see bad attitude there, not potential stalker. What about their father, Constantine's son?"

"He was your typical child of privilege, educated in England. He maintains a low profile within the corporation, but then they all do that. We couldn't determine where any of them are based at the moment, so tracking them's a challenge."

"You could talk to Constantine. You know where he is."

"We're working on that. Next up, R.J. Wilkie. Any common threads?"

"One brief meeting, then snap, he was gone. Wife, kids, friends were all stunned."

"What about his coworkers?"

"Their reactions varied. Most of them were shocked. A few suggested another woman. One said he was—"

"Abducted by aliens," a familiar voice inserted.

It seemed to Darcy that Marlowe appeared out of thin air. Although in a place where the shadows outnumbered the tables, that probably wasn't saying much.

"We're rerunning the short list of stalker suspects." Val took a longer drink this time. "In other words, we're chasing our tails. Any luck on your end?"

"I talked to Comet. Remains to be seen what develops there." Elbows propped, Marlowe pressed the heels of his hands to his eyes.

He looked tired, Darcy thought. Which only added to the appeal. A two-day growth of stubble; a black Polo shirt; faded, fitted jeans… She could get entangled all too easily—and more than willingly, given half a chance.

The already low lights dimmed. "Showtime." Val grinned. "You're in for a rare treat, Darcy darling. It's mud-wrestling night."

She hoisted her shoulder bag. "This might be a good time for me to freshen up."

Marlowe trapped her hand before she could leave. "There and back, okay? No detours to help old ladies."

Leaning over, Darcy kissed him full on the mouth.

The gleam in his eyes came and went so fast she might have imagined it. Then Val shouted, Marlowe released her and a series of strobe lights altered everything.

On her way through the crowd, the flickering lights played tricks on her, showing her an image of a faceless stalker, one whose voice had an over-the-top Tennessee accent and whose abduction MO ran to blindsiding and chloroform.

Inside the dingy washroom, a woman banged her fist on one of two closed stall doors.

"Move it. The show's started, and I gotta pee." She turned to Darcy. "Get in line. The other one's out of order." She banged again, then asked, "Can you see under the bottom? I'm not wearing my contacts, and I swear she's tripping in there."

Darcy bent to look. The second she spied the sneakers she knew it wasn't an addict inside.

Surging upright, she grabbed the angry woman's wrist. "Stop shouting. Come with me."

But it was too late. The stall door burst open, and a man flew out.

He knocked the woman aside with his left arm and with the gun in his right, blasted the overhead lights.

Darcy made it to the door, but no farther. The man slammed into her and held her against the frame.

"It's you and me now, babe," he huffed in her ear. "Like it was always meant to be. We're gonna end this thing tonight. Be glad it's going down this way, Darcy doll, 'cause if your P.I. stays out of my way for once, he might actually live to see New York again."

Darcy sucked in what air she could, told herself not to struggle or panic. If she stayed limp, he might think she'd hit her head.

"Oh, you are a smart little cookie," he cooed. He lifted her hair with his gun, rubbed the tip over her cheek. "Always thinking."

Apparently he wasn't falling for the injury.

She hissed when he pressed harder. "I can't…breathe," she said through her teeth.

"So sorry, darling," he apologized, but didn't back off. His arm snapped up and out. "Move from the floor, and you're dead, slut. Doctors say I'm a cat in the dark. It's in the genes. Move again, and I'll put a bullet in your heart. This little dance is between me and the Darcy doll." The gun returned to stroke her neck. "I like the name Darcy, maybe better than Shannon. But then I'm touching Darcy. I never did touch Shannon."

"If you like me, you'll let me breathe."

"If I let you breathe, you might wiggle your pretty self around and nail me in the balls. She cat, that's what you are. A tigress." He sniffed her neck, made her shudder. "My perfect match."

He went taut against her, and she heard the fury in his tone as his arm jerked back up. "You so much as slide your foot on the floor again, bitch, and you're dead. D'you hear—"

The rest of the question emerged as a loud *oomph* that had his breath whooshing out and his hat falling over his face.

The elbow she'd freed plunged lower the second time, a vicious jab to the stomach. She followed it up by ramming her heel down on his instep.

The gun dropped and skidded. She would have gone for it, but he caught her by the hair and flung her aside. Unbalanced, Darcy toppled first into the trash can and then into the wall. By the time her vision cleared, both man and gun were gone.

On her hands and knees, her companion screamed. Frightened, but not hurt, Darcy judged.

She ran for the door. Another woman about to enter yelped when they collided.

Darcy swung her around. "Did a man run past you?"

"More like a locomotive. He smashed into me and took off that way."

"Into the main room?"

"Guess so." Her scowl became a snicker. "It's okay, though. His hat fell off, so I got even by stomping on it."

Darcy's searching eyes located the flattened black hat with the once broad, now broken brim.

"Thanks." She glanced at the woman still screaming behind her. "Can you help her?"

"Maybe. What's she on? Hey, don't leave me..."

Her voice faded into the blare of whistles, cheers and catcalls from the predominantly male crowd. Darcy was searching the tables when a pair of hands descended on her shoulders.

"It's me," Marlowe said in her ear.

Willing her heart back into her chest, Darcy spun around. "He was in a stall. He ran out. I think he came in here."

Marlowe stared for a moment, then propelled her back toward the washrooms. "Val," he shouted over the noise. "Guy's here."

Val, who was just emerging from the same corridor as Darcy, swiveled his head. "Where?"

They all searched. For who, Darcy wasn't sure. Until…

"There." When a group of men moved, another group became visible. "Behind the stage. It's the baseball-cap guy. Damn!" She snatched her finger back. "He saw me."

"Stay here," Marlowe said. And he took off.

Beside her, Val hesitated, till Darcy assured him, "I'll be fine in the crowd." He followed his friend.

The mud-covered women in the ring circled each other like cats. Their wary movements brought to mind her attacker's remark. Doctors had compared him to a cat in the dark. Key word: *doctors.*

Would knowing he'd probably been in therapy help them?

At the moment, Darcy couldn't see how, but then her head was still reeling.

Medical records could be accessed and investigated by the police. So, she recalled suddenly, could a certain hat.

The air smelled of mud, sweat and beer as she forged a path through an increasingly boisterous crowd, back to the washrooms.

The hat was there, kicked to one side and badly crushed, but retrievable in one piece.

When she returned to the main room, she found herself scanning for exits. Like it or not—and

Marlowe wouldn't—it wasn't in her nature to stand by idly and wait.

He and Val had used the side exit. If she took the front, she might spot the guy again, see his car, get a plate number.

Sights set, she worked her way toward the main entrance. She was ten feet from the door when a clawlike hand captured her wrist and jerked her to a halt.

"Hold up there, blondie," a rusty voice warned. "You ain't goin' nowhere without me."

HE HAD HIS YANKEES CAP on backward, but it was the same guy. Marlowe had seen enough of his face to be sure of it.

He wore all black, from T-shirt to sneakers. That might have made him more difficult to track through the network of interconnecting alleys he'd chosen for his escape if Marlowe's adrenaline level and his resolve hadn't been at a peak.

The alley bottlenecked into a single lane of foot traffic but broadened near the end. After a jog, it opened onto a busy street.

The man jumped over one trash bag, landed on another and fell. Gun drawn and with no one else in sight, Marlowe fired a warning shot.

Scrambling to his feet, the man continued to run. When he reached the jog, he wove from side to side. He skirted a man climbing into a Dumpster and hopped over a junkie who was propped up like a rag doll against a dirty brick wall.

Stuffing his gun into his waistband, Marlowe followed. Baseball Cap stole a look over his shoulder as he wrapped a hand around the brick corner and used it to aid his left turn.

"Not this time, bastard," Marlowe said softly.

The traffic noise increased. A horn blared. Marlowe reached the corner, swung around it— and gave a feral smile when he realized the guy had been brought up short by a temporary fence surrounding a torn-up sidewalk.

Nowhere to run now except onto the street. The busy street, where every out-of-sorts driver in the city appeared to have congregated.

It didn't surprise him that the man took his chances. He rushed out in front of a taxi, ignored a stream of curses, then spun into the next lane.

Marlowe did the same.

The man swerved, attempted to vault over a low sports car. But the driver was young and erratic and he whipped his vehicle to the right. Tagging the man's hip, the car knocked his feet out from under him.

Marlowe pulled his gun and advanced straight-armed. "It's over, pal. Don't move."

The fallen man licked nervous lips. He started to stand. Then he spied a break in the traffic and went for it.

Marlowe knew the man wouldn't make it. The truck was approaching too fast, and with a cell phone wedged between ear and shoulder while he munched on a loaded burger, the driver had no chance to react.

The front end struck the man in the side, sending him airborne for a good ten feet. He landed shoulder first in a heap.

Marlowe lowered his gun and yanked out his cell.

"Pedestrian down," he told the 911 operator. "Unconscious. Bleeding heavily."

The hand clap on his back didn't distract him as he related the street name and block number. Breathing hard, Val motioned for him to continue while he took charge of crowd control.

"Darcy'll be okay," he called back. "I had to follow you. You know how it works."

"Yeah, I know."

With paramedics en route and Val directing traffic, Marlowe checked the fallen man's neck for a pulse. He found one, but it was thready and fast.

When a street patrol arrived, Val returned to crouch beside him. "How's he doing?"

"Hanging on." Without moving the man, Marlowe studied the gun that was strapped to his ankle.

"His face is pretty messed up." Val frowned slightly when he noticed his friend's expression. "What is it?"

Stashing his own gun, Marlowe reran the incident in the park near Darcy's place. He nodded at the injured man's leg. "Guy's carrying a Glock."

"Yeah, so?"

"The bullet that winged me last week came from a Ruger."

Chapter Fourteen

"Here we go," Val cautioned cheerfully. "PO'd female at twelve o'clock. You're a dead man."

Judging by the look on Darcy's face, Marlowe had a strong feeling he might be. She strode out of the club and across the street to stuff two balled fists into his stomach.

"Do you have any idea how tired I am of being grabbed, groped, bullied and shoved?" Without turning her head, she pointed a finger at Comet trotting a prudent five feet behind her. "He nearly scared me to death. One more hand clamps on to my arm, and I swear I'm going to chop it off. Whose brilliant idea was it to sic Comet on me any—" Her eyes widened in alarm when she noticed Marlowe's red-splattered jeans. "Is that blood? Did he shoot you?"

"No. It's the cap guy's blood. He was hit by a truck. He's on his way to the hospital."

"Is he alive?"

"For the moment."

"Do you know who he is?"

"There was no ID in his pockets," Val revealed. "Only a couple of twenties and some change. We'll run his fingerprints, maybe get lucky."

Although impassive expressions had always been his stock in trade, when Darcy drew back to regard him through her lashes, Marlowe wondered if he might be slipping.

"What aren't you telling me?" she asked.

He motioned at Comet, who saluted them and melted into the crowd. With his thumb, he erased a smudge from her cheek. "Let's just say I'm starting to wish like hell that Vince and Frankie Maco really were behind this."

A PATROL CAR FOLLOWED Darcy home. Discreetly, but she knew it was there. Just as she knew the officers inside would remain on watch until Marlowe asked Val's captain to remove them.

Damon Marlowe must have been one good cop in his time. Blydon was bending over backward to accommodate him.

Which brought to mind the question of why he'd quit. Had he been driven to it by circumstances in general, or by one particular incident? Did he ever plan to tell her about the mysterious Lisa Val had mentioned? Should she push and ask, or wait and let him volunteer the information?

For the moment at least, it was a moot point. Marlowe, Val and Blydon had rendezvoused at the hospital, where they would undoubtedly remain until either the doctors sent them on their way, the injured man regained consciousness, or he died.

In spite of his actions, Darcy didn't wish him dead. Preferably the baseball-cap guy would go to jail and she and Marlowe would wind up…together? That seemed as unlikely as the hospitalized man being an innocent bystander in this horror story.

"Okay, enough," she said out loud. Switching off the engine of Marlowe's Land Rover, she collected her gear and hopped out.

Across the street, Hannah Brewster raised a second-floor window. Mindless of the fact that it was after 10 p.m., she yelled, "It's nice to see you, dear. You've been away more than you've been home lately. How was Atlantic City?"

"It was good," Darcy returned at a more reasonable level. "Hot."

"Wonderful. Oh, I'm going to have Cristian paint your house. Is that all right with you?"

"It's fine, Mrs. B." She smiled. "Good night."

"Wait. Darcy?" Her landlady flapped a hand. "I baked an almond–wheat germ cake today."

In this heat? Darcy eased her cotton top away from her midsection. "That's nice, I guess."

"I'll send Cristian over with a generous portion for you and Marlowe."

"That's very kind of you, Mrs. B. Good night again."

Cupping both hands to her mouth, Hannah shouted a final, "You have a good evening, you hear?"

"Me and everyone else in the neighborhood," Darcy murmured.

Several yards away, an unmarked police car rolled to a halt. Strange, she thought in mild amusement, but a part of her preferred the idea of Marlowe's transplanted informant hanging out in her bushes over a pair of cops parked at the curb.

Adjusting her myriad shoulder straps, she started up the porch steps.

"Darcy?"

Now Cristian called to her, though not as volubly as Mrs. Brewster.

Balancing a plate in his hand, he cast a backward look at the boardinghouse. "I don't know what's gotten into Aunt Hannah tonight. She's been glued to that window ever since I got home. I thought she was watching for me, but I guess not."

He held out the plate as she disengaged the

alarm. "I hate to say it but this is the weirdest cake I've ever tasted. Mr. Hancock helped her make it, and it still came out funny. Real food's better, don't you think? Chocolate, ice cream, peanut butter…" He blinked at the smile she sent him. "What? You don't like real food?"

"Oh, I love it." Darcy used her hip to open the door. "Chocolate most of all. I'm just not sure I remember how it tastes." Sidetracked by a sound, she peered past Cristian. "Did you hear that?"

He glanced over. "No, I…" Then he swung around when the bushes behind him crackled. "But I heard that." He bent forward, squinted. "Could be a cat. They like to roam at night."

So did certain rodents, Darcy reflected, some of whom were human.

"Guess we should look, huh?" Cristian said when another branch snapped.

Depositing her laptop, shoulder bag and camera next to the cake, Darcy accompanied him down the porch stairs to the shrubs that separated her yard from the neighbor's.

"I couldn't cut this hedge down," he whispered. "Aunt Hannah wanted me to, but it's on the other side of the property line and— Holy crap!"

This as Podge launched out of the bushes, feet first and yowling.

A shocked Cristian caught him, but immediately let go. "Wow! Uh, wow!" His laugh was tinged with nervous embarrassment. "Sorry. I didn't expect that."

Darcy calmed her racing heart. "Neither did I."

Within seconds, Hannah Brewster was hastening across the street in her muumuu, breathlessly calling for Podge to calm down and stop making such a fuss.

Braving the cat's wrath, she picked him up. He scratched her twice, but she maintained her grip, holding the wriggling animal at arm's length.

"I'm so, so sorry," she apologized to Darcy. "He's been a crotchety beast all day. I'll take him home and lock him in the cellar." She extended her arms a little more. "Cristian dear, do you mind?"

Clearly unenthused, her nephew reached out a tentative hand. When the animal didn't swipe at him, he ventured cautiously, "You can probably put him down, Aunt Hannah. Whatever spooked him, he's getting over it."

Darcy allowed the cat to sniff her fingers. "It's okay, Mrs. B, you can leave him here."

Hannah's eyes touched on the distant cruiser. "Could be he caught his tail on a branch." She summoned a smile. "I'll go back home, then." A light winked on across the street in one of the second-floor bedrooms. Her smile relaxed. "Yes indeed, I'll do that. Cristian, you come as well.

I'll fix you some cake and iced tea." She patted Darcy's hand. "Good night, dear. Sleep well."

Darcy waited until they were gone to stare down at Podge, now calmly washing his face at her feet. "Okay, that was weird, right? I mean, it wasn't just me."

Before going inside, she glanced at the boardinghouse and visualized a garrote being snapped in a short-order cook's strong hands.

Then tipping her head to the side, she regarded the tall stand of cedars that ran along the entire west side of her own house.

WHILE DARCY DISLIKED hospitals, Marlowe hated them. Being in one set his teeth on edge. So it came as no surprise that by 1:00 a.m., he wanted to shove his fist into something. Or someone.

Since that someone was under no circumstances going to be Darcy, he got Val to drop him in the park so he could walk it off.

He'd looked in on Matilda tonight. She was conscious, but ornery and disinclined to talk to the police. Darcy might have better luck. Persuading people to talk was her job. And from what he'd seen and read, she did that job very well.

She did a lot of things well, actually. Topping the list right now was sex. With crisis management only slightly below it.

Another small step down, but no less amazing to him, was her ability to harness her journalistic nature. She could easily have dug into his past. That she hadn't spoke volumes about her character and far more about her heart than he was prepared to acknowledge.

At the sound of scurrying footsteps, Marlowe let the ghost of a smile cross his lips.

"Hey, Comet," he greeted without turning. "Got something for me?"

"Got a parched throat and nothing to wet it down at my flop."

The smile became a chuckle. "Will fifty help?"

"You always was generous." The little man fell into step beside him. "Okay, here's the dope. Guy you lit out after tonight came into the club after you. Word is he hung at the bar the whole time till you flushed him out."

"Whose word?"

Comet's bearded mouth split into a nicotine-stained smile. "Lady I talked to. She says the guy never left the bar, just watched the three of you. Looked at the clock when the pretty lady got up, but didn't follow her right away. By the time he did make a move in that direction, pretty lady was coming back out. Then she saw him, and you saw him and he took off, lickety-split."

Marlowe pulled five twenties from his pocket

while he processed the information. "You did good tonight, Comet. Rates a bonus."

The little man stuffed the money into his shirt. "Just sniffed around some and watched after the pretty lady like you asked. Weren't no hardship." Comet eyeballed him from the side. "Saw her give you a mashed-up hat. Did it tell you anything?"

"Yeah, it told me something. I'm not sure yet if it was something I wanted to hear."

DARCY WORKED ON HER laptop until she heard Marlowe come in. Shutting down, she stood, gave her hair a shake and strolled to the second-floor railing. With her forearms resting on the polished wood, she watched him reset the alarm.

"I hope you're not thinking about staying down there tonight, Mr. Investigator. My sofa's nice, but it's not meant to be slept on…if that's your intention." Pushing back, she started down the stairs. "Now if it turns out it is, let me say that I have a slightly more…provocative suggestion." With her hair spilling over the side of her face, she set her tongue on her upper lip and in a single, smooth movement, let her robe drop to the floor.

She kept coming, lowering her eyes to the front of his jeans and allowing a sparkle to swim up. "Now that," she noted, "is a very promising sign."

On the second-to-last step, she arched a guile-less brow. "Cat got your tongue, Marlowe? Or is it that there's nothing you want to say? Only things—" she descended another step, took the rock-hard front of his jeans in her hands "—you want to do." Replacing her hands with her hips, she shimmied against him, brought her mouth closer to his. "I don't know about you, but I'm in the mood for a fire."

His mesmerizing eyes didn't waver from hers. "Fires consume, Darcy. Can you handle that?"

With his hands cradling her, she wrapped a single leg around him, kissed him long and deep. A brow went up as she drew back.

"Enough of an answer for you, Marlowe?"

"Not even close," he said. Crushing his mouth to hers, he let the flames erupt.

No! He walked in circles.

No! He karate-chopped the air.

No! He pounded his fists on the wall.

She was his. She would be his. He was done play-acting.

Feeble, that's what he'd been. But no more. No show of mercy to the P.I. The slimeball was trying to steal his woman!

Pow, pow. Two shots would take him down. The first was for pain. You think the Darcy doll can hurt you with her knee? Just wait until your balls meet my gun. Ooh, man, it's gonna sting. He'd see to that…

Right before bullet number two got him between the eyes.

Mustn't forget, though, Darcy was the goal. No victory in drilling the P.I. if he couldn't carry out his plan for her.

Gotta set priorities, he reminded himself. Stick to them… Shut up, he warned the yappy doctor voices in his head. Bunch of quacks. You can't fix it if it ain't broke, people. What? You think it's broken? You think I'm broken? Man, are you dumb. Dumber than dumb. Why am I even talking to you? Go home to your pools and your Porsches, your martinis and your mistresses. I've got work to do.

"Gonna get my woman at long, long last," he promised out loud. "Gonna make her mine forever."

Grabbing a pen, he drew a heart around one of the photographs that adorned the wall in front of him.

"Gonna love you to death, pretty Darcy doll."

SEX WITH MARLOWE WAS like a dream in the middle of her worst nightmare.

They made love three times. They ordered pizza at 4:00 a.m. They talked until after six.

He told her more than she expected to hear.

He'd gone to Michigan State, had been a wide receiver from his sophomore year until graduation. He'd majored in criminology and political science.

He'd had two serious relationships in his life. Neither had worked, but the second one had been the worst.

Long story short, he'd been addicted to his career.

Darcy wondered which one was the Lisa that Val had mentioned. Lucky for him, she'd given her word not to ask.

As good things tended to, the night ended much too soon. With the dawn came a phone call from Val. Forensics had double-checked the decimated hat and come up with seventeen hair types and dozens of skin and saliva samples. Evidently, the club floors weren't cleaned very often.

Marlowe left to meet him in Center City.

Feeling revved, Darcy considered going in to the magazine—until she realized that whatever needed doing could be done by e-mail.

She zipped off the article Elaine had requested the previous day, added an outline for a fall feature and said she'd be back in the office tomorrow.

She spent most of the morning up in her ninety-eight-degree attic, going through old storage boxes. She was on the third one and debating whether to continue or set fire to the room when a horn blasted rudely outside.

"Lovely." Dropping her head back, she watched dust particles dance in a slanting sunbeam. "Mohammad comes to the mountain."

Two minutes later, hands on hips and tapping an impatient foot, Elaine stood in the middle of the attic. "You call this doing research? If that's the case, you can come over to my place tomorrow and do your research in my garage."

Not waiting for a response, she strode from door to window, raising angry puffs of dust as she went.

Darcy waited. Watched. "Uh, Elaine?"

"I fired him," her boss snapped. She whipped her head around. "Did you hear me? I did what I had to do for the sake of the magazine. I did what any sane employer would do, and yet I feel guilty. Why is that, Darcy? Why?"

"Well, I suppose—"

"I caught him in the women's washroom again. That's two times in less than a week. He was hiding in one of the stalls with his cell phone. What was I supposed to do? Tell me, please, because I'm driving myself crazy here."

Darcy set aside a torn manila envelope. "You could insist he get help, go for counseling."

"He won't do it."

"He will if he values his career. And he should. As far as I'm aware, this is the best job he's had since he graduated from college."

"Trace hates doctors. Hates them," Elaine emphasized.

Hated doctors? That tidbit roused her curiosity. The guy in the washroom last night said he hated doctors. "How do you know that?" Darcy asked.

"Because he's been to dozens of them. He's been hospitalized twice. Intervention by his mother. I mean, come on, you had to figure, right? The guy's a walking blob of angst, fetishes and major neuroses."

Momentarily sidetracked by a photo that had spilled from the envelope, Darcy brought her eyes and her mind back. "In other words, he's totally screwed up."

"Nail on the head, kiddo. Artistically brilliant, but socially stunted."

Standing, Darcy worked a cramp from her calf. "Where is he now?"

"I haven't the foggiest." Pausing by the window, her editor stared through the pane. "As a point of interest, did you know there's a man skulking around outside?"

"Really?" Darcy went to the window. "That's

John Hancock." She watched him pass by on the far side of the street. "I see a vulture searching for a carcass."

"Not a friend of yours, I take it."

"Neighbor."

"What's his line? Is he a burglar in training?"

Darcy's smile was distant. "Short-order cook, or so he says. He's looking for work."

"Seems more like he's looking for you. He's gone past your place four times since I got here."

"Wonder how he feels about doctors," Darcy murmured with a glance at the picture on the floor behind her.

"Should I understand that question?"

"I'm not sure I do." She turned from the window. "But before this day's over, I intend to."

SHE LOCATED MARLOWE at police headquarters. He was using Val's computer and had disks and papers scattered everywhere.

"One more item for your pile, Marlowe." Bending over an empty corner of the desk, Darcy dangled the photo she'd discovered in her attic. "Red heart drawn around Shannon's head as she walks through hotel lobby. No big deal, I thought back in the day. Except this morning, for the first time, I noticed a squiggle on the tip of the heart. It's a match for the squiggle on the headstone he sent me, which, tit for tat, I didn't notice until I saw this one."

Marlowe examined the photo. "This guy's been watching you for a while, Darcy."

"Comforting thought, huh? I calculated the dates. Between my on-air job in Oregon and this photo, the time frame's roughly two and a half years."

"What other gifts did you receive during that time?"

"Roses, candy, some porcelain dolls, which I donated to a children's charity. Various pieces of jewelry, also donated, and a handblown Italian glass sculpture."

"Of?"

She fought to keep the shudder at bay. "A woman and a man intertwined and rising out of a waterfall. It's interpretive, and at the time I thought, quite lovely."

"Do you still have it?"

"Lovely," she repeated, "but too delicate for my gypsy lifestyle. I gave it to my godmother. It's in her curio cabinet in Switzerland."

"And you just remembered it now."

She met his stare across the desk. "Marlowe, I told you, people in the media receive gifts." She breathed out, gave in. "I also told you one of my coworkers in Los Angeles had a stalker after her."

"Why am I sensing a *but?*"

She sighed. "A possible *but*. Looking back, I'm not sure the stalker was after her. It could've been me."

"Because?"

"Thing's used to appear on her desk. Logically, we assumed they were meant for her. Except we switched desks after our first week together. What we didn't bother to switch were the nameplates attached to them. And I do mean attached. They were screwed into the wood on the front. But no mail or files ever got mixed up because our coworkers knew she kept a big bowl of lavender potpourri next to her computer. Bowl on top, must be Emma's desk. It's called visual reference. Coworkers used it. I doubt a stalker would."

"But the gifts stopped coming, right?"

A chill rippled through her. "Six months before she left. A year before the Maco trial and Shannon Hunt's disappearance."

Still facing her across the desk, Marlowe took her hands and ran his thumbs lightly over her knuckles. "Let me get the time frame straight. There were approximately two and a half years of gifts and cards that could have been stalker-related, then a year of nothing."

"Yes. Nothing as well for the last three years. Then suddenly, Umer Lugo hired you to find me.

The guy in the washroom last night mentioned doctors. It's possible he was hospitalized for a time."

Marlowe brought her up with him as he stood. His hypnotic gold eyes stared into hers. "We'll figure it out, Darcy. I'm running every name I can think of through the system."

She found she could still laugh. "Well, that's a relief. Or would be if I had any faith at all in the system."

He touched her cheek. "It has its moments."

"That would be my cue to ask if you've found something."

A gleam appeared in his eyes. "Blydon ran the baseball-cap guy through California police and prison records and came up with the name Ivan Kazarov."

"Sorry, no lightbulbs. Does he have a background?"

"He has an occupation."

"Which is?"

Marlowe kept his eyes on her face while he kissed the palm of her hand. "He's what's known in cop circles as a hit man."

Chapter Fifteen

The story was getting better and better, Darcy thought later that day. Someone had sent a hit man after her. Not the most efficient one in the world, but a hired killer nonetheless.

Ivan Kazarov had a record and a reputation. The rep was for murder, unfortunately never proven. The record involved a sloppily executed robbery for which he'd served four years in California State Prison.

He'd been released two months ago. Perhaps through default, he'd turned to private investigation. At least he called it that. If he had clients, however, there was no list available since he worked out of a studio apartment in East L.A. and didn't appear to keep records.

As a favor to Blydon, the police agreed to search his home. It was late afternoon by the time he received word that they'd come up empty.

For the remainder of the day, Marlowe alternated between his laptop and Val's computer while Val and two sets of uniformed guards hung out at the hospital. Darcy stayed at the station, too, using her own laptop to source any and all media-related stories. Frustration set in when she hit her twenty-third wall.

Barefoot, she did a long yoga stretch and endeavored to sort through the clutter of useless details she'd unearthed.

"R.J. Wilkie liked bloodhounds, ghost towns and *Seinfeld* reruns," she said while she worked her muscles. "He admired P.T. Barnum, Walt Disney and Indira Gandhi. Odd but interesting combination. His mother's still alive. His father died from cancer six months before he disappeared. It makes me think motive for vanishing act, but doesn't really connect to this situation."

Marlowe sat back, took a drink from Darcy's water bottle. "Anything on Hickey's son?"

"Only that he's thirty-three, has a plethora of personal problems and is totally camera-shy. There isn't a single picture of him that I could find on record. There's the one Val discovered, and others like it—of him in full stage makeup— so maybe with the right program he could be taken from character to man, but my computer doesn't have that capability."

"Police computer does."

"Right. Your job, then." Rotating her shoulder, she let the tension in her neck and spine flow away. "As far as Constantine Lyons is concerned, there's not much. The family is private almost to a fault. Except for the eldest grandson whose auto-racing career is starting to hum after more than seven years of mediocre results. There is one thing, though. Constantine's son is rumored to have a serious psychological disorder."

"Yeah, I got that, too." Marlowe took another drink, offered her the bottle when she returned to center. "Any idea what kind?"

"Schizophrenia was mentioned more than once. Snippets of other stories suggest he's spent more time being treated in London and Paris than he has piloting the board of Constantine's corporation. He married a British restaurant heiress, managed to father three sons with her, brought his family back to California and was in the process of getting a divorce when his wife died. Vehicle crash on the Pacific Coast Highway. The son who was with her and survived is the one who chose auto racing as a career."

"Who was driving when she died?"

"Consensus is it was her, although both of them were thrown from their seats. As for Constantine's other two grandsons, that being the middle and the youngest, ages thirty-one and thirty respectively, the same rumor that dogs their father has also been applied to them. Mental-health issues. You might be able to go deeper there. The walls came fast and furious for me after the story about the son. Right now I'm feeling claustrophobic and cranky, which tells me I need a break." Popping her sunglasses on her head, Darcy strapped on her high-heeled sandals and picked up her shoulder bag. "Val's still at the hospital, right?"

Marlowe leaned forward. "Do you have a plan I should know about?"

"Working on it." With a sassy smile, she pulled out her cell.

Val answered on the first ring.

"Has Kazarov regained consciousness?" she asked him.

"Twice, but either he's pretending not to hear me, or his brain took a harder hit than the X-rays suggest, because we're getting squat from him. Far as I can see, there's only one avenue of attack left to us, and unfortunately you're there rather than here."

That surprised a laugh out of her. "You want me to talk to him?"

"Why not? Maybe if he sees you as a flesh-and-blood person, he'll feel a twinge of guilt. Combine that with the fact that he's under arrest and facing God knows how many charges, and he might be willing to throw us a bone. A small one would do."

Reaching around the monitor, Darcy picked up Marlowe's wrist and checked his watch. "It's almost seven. I can be there in twenty minutes."

"I'll meet you in the main parking lot."

Darcy spied the doubt in Marlowe's eyes. Grinning, she tweaked his chin. "Relax. Val's meeting me outside the hospital. You can walk me to my car. So neatly encapsulated, how could anything happen?"

"Said the iceberg to the *Titanic*." He wrapped a light hand around her throat. "My gut and our witness say it wasn't Kazarov who attacked you in the washroom last night, Darcy."

"I was there when you questioned her, remember? Come on, Marlowe, she saw you, me and more than one pink elephant during that conversation." At his level expression, she quelled a flicker of impatience. "Why don't we compromise? Comet can come to the hospital with me."

"You don't mind that?"

"Not if it gets me what I want." She leaned in close, her mouth inches away from his. "Speaking of what I want…"

She meant to close the gap between them

slowly, but Marlowe pulled her against him, chest to thigh, in one quick swoop.

His kiss sent her mind and her senses reeling.

She sighed out a breath when he raised his head. "You're some good kisser."

He smiled, and leaned in for what she thought would be another kiss. Instead, he whispered in her ear, "Don't ditch him, Darcy. Small as he is, Comet's never lost a fight."

Amusement stirred. "Don't worry. I won't test him tonight." She pressed a finger to his lower lip. "And while we're on the subject of tonight, how about I meet you at my place when you're finished here?" She nibbled his lip. "You bring the wine."

She heard the faint rumble in his throat when she ran her tongue along the side of his jaw. And laughed when his mouth came down hot and hungry on hers.

THE SKY HAD AN UNNATURAL cast to it. Darcy didn't pay much attention to the bruised and swollen clouds until she and Comet pulled into the hospital parking lot. Obviously more concerned than her, the little man hopped out, surveyed the area before he fell into step beside her.

As lightning forked down over the Delaware, she waved at Val, several yards ahead.

"How's Kazarov?" she asked when they caught up.

"Faking it, if you ask me."

"The head injury's real enough, Val."

"What about Tilda?" Comet asked.

"You know her?" Darcy and Val stared, but it was Darcy who asked, "Did you mention that to Marlowe?"

Comet shrugged. "Nothing to mention. I'm asking for a friend of mine."

Darcy smiled at Val. "Kind of surreal, isn't it? My head's spinning."

"Well, your feet are dragging," Val noted. "Don' tell me you have an aversion to hospitals, too. Honey, you and Marlowe are such a pair."

"I'd love to explore that with you, Detective, some other time." She resisted even more when he steered her to the right. "Why are we using the emergency entrance?"

"It's the fastest way in. In case you've forgotten, you've seen far worse out here lately than you're likely to encounter in there."

"Tell you what. You wheel Kazarov outside and I'll—" She broke off to stare at the side of the building. "Whoa," she said softly. "Talk about pink elephants."

Val fanned a hand in front of her face. "What is it, Darcy?"

"Val, I swear I saw someone I recognize."

"Who was it?"

She shivered off the sensation of maggots crawling down her spine. "It was Trace, I'm sure of it. I saw Trace Grogan between the bushes and the hospital wall."

HE HAD TO BACKPEDAL quickly, almost had to run.

Had she seen him? He wasn't sure. It was getting dark, and not a pretty, starlit kind of dark. Black clouds were massing over the river.

His heart thudded. Sweat pooled under his arms. A trickle of it ran down his back.

Luckily, the music pulsing in his head blotted out the worst of it. Burning, he was burning inside. Gotta make it happen tonight. Thunder and lightning were better than the moon and stars anyway. It would be wild, a sexual frenzy. And then…

His heart raced faster. A smile stole across his lips. His tongue flicked at the saliva in the corners. He wanted to tremble, but he wouldn't. No, no, have to keep it together. Have to catch her. Have to kiss her.

Have to kill her.

MARLOWE SPENT SIXTY minutes online after Darcy left. He swore there was a time bomb ticking in his head.

Sitting back, he ran a finger under his lower lip and contemplated the names on the monitor. There were no other lists on Umer Lugo's laptop. He was convinced that one of these people had wanted to locate Darcy, aka Shannon Hunt.

Not the Macos. He'd pretty much eliminated them. That left Nelda Hickey's son, a missing news anchor and one or more members of the emotionally disturbed Constantine Lyons clan.

He had no photos, no clues that made sense and no solid leads. All he had were his instincts, and he figured those had taken him as far as they could at this point.

So what was he missing? What were all of them not seeing, not realizing, not questioning?

Why were there no photos? the cop in him wondered. Why so many mystery people? Although he sensed that last thing was a coincidence, the question didn't sit well.

On the plus side, there were numerous pictures of R.J. Wilkie. The fifty-something man was or had been dark-haired with patches of distinguished gray at his temples. On paper, he came off jowly, but he'd obviously been handsome enough to make it in the off-hours television news world. Married with two teenage kids, he'd been under contract to a well-known media group when he'd vanished.

Had he also been obsessed? Marlowe didn't think so. Couldn't say why, but the idea simply didn't gel.

On to the Memphis-born impersonator. Now there was a definite possibility, right down to the Tennessee twang. Ah, but Darcy, who'd lived in a number of different states, said that twang hadn't rung true for her.

Was she right or being cleverly faked out by a man who made his living mimicking celebrity accents? Val had been told he did a killer Sinatra as well as an excellent Mick Jagger and Cher. Although it hadn't been mentioned, Marlowe imagined he could also do a damn good Elvis.

So why were there no photos of him sans stage makeup? Why, with such a famous mother, had there never been photos?

Rocking his neck from side to side, Marlowe traded one mystery for another.

Constantine Lyons and family.

The old man was proving difficult to contact. Not surprising, really, considering his advanced age and the relative buoyancy of his corporate holdings. He could afford to have legions of people running all manner of interference for him. He could more than afford to keep his son and grandsons' mental and emotional issues out of the press.

When approached, the only grandson who was accessible talked about racing and nothing else. The rest of his life was off-limits and removed from the public eye.

Val's computer beeped as a message came in from Blydon. Opening it, Marlowe saw a single name printed in caps.

HICKEY

Scrolling down, he studied the man's face. Computer techs had taken him from Ozzy to ordinary, or close enough that Marlowe would know if he'd seen the guy.

He hadn't, but then again, if Hickey could do Ozzy, Frank and Cher, who knew what other personas he might be able to adopt on a daily basis.

Feeling out of sorts and edgy, Marlowe went to the credenza to pour himself a mug of coffee.

He didn't recognize Hickey's unadorned face, and even altering it in his mind, he came up empty. Height, last known weight, build—all were average numbers at best. Similar to Kazarov, in some respects. Except that Ivan Kazarov was the genuine article, traceable from date of birth to hospital bed.

Swallowing a mouthful of coffee, Marlowe returned to the Lyons clan. Rumor suggested a disturbed son. How disturbed were they talking? Somewhat unstable or completely over the edge?

Setting the oldest grandson aside, the middle

and youngest were also questionable. No one he or Blydon had contacted in California was willing to talk about them.

Taking a last drink of bitter coffee, Marlowe regarded the ceiling tiles. "Helluva case you got me into, Lugo. One part ecstasy to nine parts crap."

Should he play with fire and let the ecstasy rule? Or stay focused on the crap and the danger that wormed through it? Danger that felt close enough to touch. Close enough to snap its jaws on the woman he…

Whoa.

Marlowe brought the mug down with a jerk. What had he almost thought? *Love?* Was that the word? The feeling? The truth?

His blood ran cold at the idea. But God help him, it might be true.

Lowering his gaze to the floor, he ordered himself to back up. And back away, before it was too late.

He'd shut his emotions down a long, long time ago. That was his defense mechanism.

He'd screwed up his life and his head. He'd turned his back on the light and allowed the dark to take over. If he hadn't, the pain would have consumed him by now. Pain spurred by memories—of sirens and red and blue flashes, and the eerie strains of carnival music.

Of a single deadly gunshot…

He swore as he pictured the moment, brought his eyes up, let them harden. No way was Darcy going to die.

So why the hell was he still here while she was at the hospital? If he wanted to keep her safe, distance wasn't the answer.

When he started to set his mug aside, the bottom bumped against the filing cabinet. Some of the coffee sloshed over the sides.

Since Val's files were covered with stains, he wasn't overly concerned. He gave the folders a shake to dislodge the worst of the spill and set them on a shelf to dry.

He would have left it at that if the name on the third folder hadn't caught his eye. The name—and the DMV snapshot that slipped out to land on the credenza.

Mostly because it was turned toward him, Marlowe regarded the blown-up shot. He'd seen better, but who couldn't say that about their driver's license picture?

Instead of returning the photo to the file, however, he found himself studying it. The longer he did, the edgier he became. Something felt wrong to him, something he couldn't quite pinpoint.

He honed in on the eyes. Windows to the soul, if you believed. *Not right* was all he saw. The shape was off. Same thing with the nose and mouth. As for the ears...

The truth hit like a blow to the stomach. "Dammit!" His insides gave a single vicious twist. His throat went dry.

Shooting off from the cabinet, he grabbed his keys and his gun, checked the clock. It was closing in on eight-thirty.

Darcy would be at the hospital, would have been there for more than an hour by now. Sixty-plus minutes, in a large building, with corridors that crisscrossed like a maze and a reduced night staff probably already in place.

As he ran, he pulled out his cell, punched Darcy's name. The line was busy.

Swearing, he pushed past a man in cuffs and two more with black eyes. He hit Blydon's number and the stairs simultaneously, but had to slow to a jog as he approached the entrance.

An incoming group of people, police and civilians, blocked the doorway.

Blydon didn't answer. Pressing his phone off, Marlowe wedged himself through on the side. He would have made it if a woman in the back hadn't separated herself from the officer next to her and rushed over to wrap the fingers of both hands around his arm.

Sobbing hysterically, she threw herself against his chest.

Chapter Sixteen

"Said blue shoes. Sang it, sort of. Did a dance. Then he got mad and knocked me down. I thought he was gonna do me. Something stopped him. Grabbed my cart. Shoved it. Took off."

Matilda's voice resembled sandpaper. Her knobby fingers worried her hospital blanket. She stared for a moment before her eyes left Darcy's face and went to the curtained wall in front of her.

"Seen that look before. Crazy man. Got no feeling 'cept for what he wants. Gonna get it no matter what. Said he'd do me later. That's all I remember. Watched my cart run away, then the park went fuzzy."

Darcy showed her the police drawing of Ivan Kazarov. "Was this the man you saw, Matilda?"

The old woman rocked back and forth against her pillow. "Saw him, yeah. Didn't stop, just ran past like the devil was after him. Saw three men, all running. Tallest one was best. He yours?"

"Not exactly…"

"You want him to be yours, I bet. Don't blame you." She rocked some more, then stopped and reached out a finger to touch Darcy's hair. "Pretty," she said. "Soft." Her vision clouded. "Keep seeing blue shoes. Both times I saw him, singing 'bout blue shoes."

Darcy let her touch, but patted her wrist to keep her on track. "Was the song 'Blue Suede Shoes,' Matilda?"

A wispy smile revealed large gaps between the old woman's teeth. "Singing like Elvis. I remember it now. Blue shoes…"

She started to hum. Because it seemed to make her happy, Darcy motioned for Comet to stay there while she slipped away to join Val on the other side of the curtain.

"This isn't telling us anything," he muttered. "We already know about the Elvis deal."

"We also know that Kazarov isn't the person who attacked her. Which means—" she shivered "—he's not the one who's been attacking me."

"What we have, Darcy, is a lunatic with a weird proclivity for Elvis and a guy with a mystery agenda who appears to be a New York Yankees fan. Doesn't exactly make the picture any clearer."

"It separates some of the elements. Matilda said, 'Both times I saw him, singing about blue shoes.' Both times, Val. When he stole her cart and used it to try and knock Marlowe down, and again when he attacked her in the parking lot at the street shelter. Same song, same guy."

"Same guy, same no description. Unless there's someone out there singing 'Blue Suede Shoes' constantly, we still can't put a face to whoever's after you. I suppose we could go with Trace Grogan, except no one's actually seen him, in the hospital or on the grounds."

"I saw him."

He held up a hand. "I believe you. I'm just saying."

Darcy heard her cell phone ring. However, when she reached into her shoulder bag, it wasn't there. Had she left it on Matilda's bed?

The ringing stopped. She glanced at the curtain. "Do you still want me to talk to Kazarov?"

Val rubbed a bloodshot eye. "If the orderlies ever finish changing his sheets."

"It's been over thirty minutes. I'm sure they're done by now. Give me a second, okay?" Stepping around the curtain, she found Matilda still singing to herself and Comet cheerfully chatting to someone on her cell phone.

"Don't you worry about her. I'm here, and so are the cops. We won't let no one kill her." He looked over, grinned. "Here she is now. You can talk to her yourself."

Darcy took the phone. "Who is it?"

"Said she's your godmother."

She winced and took a deep breath. "Nana, hi…No, that wasn't a new boyfriend… No, we haven't been drinking. I'm sorry, I haven't got much time, but here's a brief version of the story…"

HE KNEW EXACTLY WHERE to go. He knew exactly what to do. Opportunity was what he needed now.

Marlowe wasn't here. Too bad about that, but he'd still suffer when she was dead—assuming he loved her, and he probably did.

"Gonna leave you all shook up, Mr. P.I. Gonna make the Darcy doll mine forever."

Excitement simmered. He prepped his gun, stuffed it into his pants, rearranged his top to cover it and took a last walk around the seventh floor.

Spotting a stationary trolley, he snagged one of the items on top. When the song started up in his head, he began to get hard.

LIKE THE GUARD OUTSIDE Matilda's door, the officer watching Kazarov gave Comet a strange look as he scuttled past. Waving him off, Val ushered Darcy and the little man into the room.

"Give me a minute. I seem to have lost some patrolmen."

From behind Darcy's shoulder, Comet sneered. "Guy don't look like a killer to me."

Darcy cocked her head at the man whose eyes remained firmly shut. "Is there a specific look associated with the hit world?"

"Yeah, and it's tougher than a has-been boxer with a cauliflower ear and a bent nose."

Perching on the bed, she leaned over Kazarov. "I work with a guy who pretends to be asleep almost as well as you do, Mr. Kaarov. I recognize the signs."

A pulse jumped in Kazarov's neck. Without opening his eyes, he offered a reedy, "Call me dead meat, sweetheart, 'cause that's what I'm gonna be soon enough. Old Conly'll see to that."

"Who's Old Conly?" Darcy asked.

"Boss man." Kazarov began to drift. "Knew I was crap as a killer. Only ever did one guy, and I got lucky with him. Heart wasn't in it, Conly said. Hired me as a backup to his lawyer. Lugo went with the safe bet. He figured once he had you flushed out, he could do the rest. But outfox a crazy fox? Nuh-uh, Umer, don't think so. And I was right. There's Lugo, floating in a tub, and his mission's nowhere near complete. Maybe things are even worse now. Enter me. The big screwup."

Kazarov's slurry voice faded in and out. "But I got ideas. Oh, yeah. I've got a plan to flush and trap."

Comet tugged her arm. "Mind if I find a bathroom?" he whispered.

"No, go ahead." She studied Kazarov's face. "Are you still awake?"

"Yeah. Lotta painkillers. Lotta pain."

Unsure how hard to push, Darcy continued. "It isn't that I'm not grateful, but why are you telling me all this and not the police?"

A laugh gurgled out. "Feel like I know you. Maybe feel bad, too. Got a kid myself, a girl. Don't see her much. Thirteen. Pretty kid. Blonde, like you. Hope she lives longer."

Fear bounced from Darcy's stomach to her throat. "Longer than who?" she asked.

He laughed again, wetter this time. "Your P.I., me, the old lady down the hall. Whoever. Doesn't matter to him how many die. Eye on the prize. That's you."

More thunder rumbled beyond the window. Darcy harnessed her nerves. "Who is he?" she pressed. "Kazarov, I need a name."

He coughed thickly when he laughed. Except he wasn't really laughing, and recognizing the difference made Darcy's palms go damp.

"Ethan," he burbled. "Name's Ethan Lyons."

Her heart gave several hard thumps. "Constantine Lyons," she murmured. "You call him Conly."

"Smart girl," Kazarov congratulated her. "Smarter still if you run straight from here to the cop shop. Really thought my plan'd work. Watch you, and the problem child would show. Catch him cold, bring him back, hush it up, bury it deep."

"Bring him back to his father or his grandfather?"

Kazarov ignored her question and continued his rambling story.

"Really good plan. Solid. But you and the P.I. kept screwing me up, so I could never follow him. Still not sure where he's hiding out. Saw him near your house once, then, snap, gone." He croaked out a chuckle. "Should've known I'd never catch him in the dark. Cat vision. Can't beat that at night."

"Cat vision." Darcy sifted through her memories of the attack in the bar washroom. "He told me he had cat vision," she recalled. "He said it was in the genes."

"Old man's was like a cat's. Still has the predatory instincts, just not the eyes. Kid's got 'em, though."

"Kid. His kid?"

Kazarov sucked in a sudden breath. "Damn,

that hurts. Hot knife… Grandkid," he said through clenched teeth.

"Which one? Kazarov, tell me, which grandson?"

"Youngest. Brain's bad. So bad."

Darcy searched for the call button. She followed the line under the sheet, but couldn't pry it out of his fingers. "Let go, and I'll press it for you."

"Hot knife," he said again. Darcy heard thunder, felt his body tighten. His fingers maintained their death grip on the button.

"Kazarov," she tried again, but halted when his eyes widened in alarm.

Her own eyes locked on his chest beneath the sheet. She felt her breath stutter as blood began to seep through the cotton.

She sensed a third presence a split second before she heard the rustle of fabric. An arm snaked around her from behind, and a brown teddy bear appeared. It had two holes in its smiling head.

"Say hello to my beautiful lady, little guy. Sorry about the bullet holes, Darcy doll, but that guard outside had to go. And I think I did your suffering friend here a favor by shooting him." His mouth moved to her ear. "It's you and me now, gorgeous. No need for cutesy props." He let the toy drop to the bed. "Turn around and kiss your real-life teddy bear."

MARLOWE DIDN'T REMEMBER much about leaving the station, only that it took far too long.

His nerves were raw, his control teetering on the brink.

The rain had come at last, and with a vengeance. Lightning split the night sky. Thunder shook the ground beneath his tires. The pavement was slick and more than one motorist had already spun into a freeway barrier.

He got through to Val on his fifth attempt, but it was a weak connection at best.

"Where's Darcy?" were the first words out of his mouth.

"She's here. Somewhere. I left her with Kazarov and your informant. There was a guard outside the door. I…" His voice cracked and with it the lie. "Aw, man, I blew it, big-time. When I ran into Comet in the washroom, I knew, I just knew something was going to happen. And it did."

Marlowe swerved around a moving van. "Where, Val?"

"I don't know. Look, I've got a seriously wounded officer and a dead hit man. I've got Security combing the corridors. Two nurses saw her with an orderly. They think they've seen him before. They gave me a description but no name."

"I've got a name." Marlowe checked the dashboard clock, forced his brain to function. "Real name, fake guy."

"You're breaking up. Fake who…?"

The line went dead. Marlowe tossed his phone aside.

This wouldn't go down at the hospital, he was sure of that. The guy had a plan, and he'd find a way to carry it out.

But where?

The question echoed in his head, so loud it almost drowned out the phone ringing beside him.

"Marlowe?" Val shouted. "Are you there?"

He came perilously close to sideswiping a van as he squealed around a corner. "She's not at the hospital, Val. Tell the uniforms to keep looking, but meet me at the boardinghouse."

"But shouldn't we be searching—"

"We are. I ran into Hannah Brewster at the station tonight. It's a long story, involving garrotes and shoes and bushes and cats. Just get in your car and meet me there. I'll be in room four, sixth door on the right, second floor."

"Got it. Fifteen minutes. Are you sure about this?"

"Yeah, I'm sure. Guy's a pretender with a whole lotta luck on his side." Squealing around another corner, Marlowe set his mind and his sights on Hannah Brewster's boardinghouse. "That luck ends tonight."

"THEY'LL FIGURE IT OUT." Darcy refused to let her voice tremble, a difficult feat with a gun pressed to the side of her neck.

He'd whisked her out of the hospital through a side exit to his waiting car. Actually, it was Hannah Brewster's car, but would a murderer care about stealing a vehicle?

He'd used the teddy bear to hide his gun and a happy-go-lucky smile to mask his insanity.

"Don't make me do it here, Darcy doll," he'd whispered as they'd walked. "I've been waiting for this for years. Got hard every night thinking about it." He'd adopted the false twang. "You're my one and only sugar pie, and I'm your U.S. male." He'd laughed, lost the twang. "You gotta love Elvis, don't you? The man had a song for every occasion." He'd kissed her cheek from behind. When she'd shuddered, he'd laughed. "I know, Darcy doll. I'm all shivery with anticipation, too…"

"Eight more blocks," he told her now.

A bolt of lightning shot to the ground. The thunder behind it made her hand shake on the steering wheel.

Despite the cloying heat, Darcy's teeth wanted to chatter. She had no idea where they were going and no way to communicate that destination to Marlowe even if she found out.

Which, unfortunately, she would before much longer.

"You drive real good, Darcy doll. I've watched you pull up to the curb lots of times. Watched you pull away, too. You like to go fast, but you're not reckless. Now, me, I'm reckless. At least the doctors say I am. But I'm careful, too. Methodical and calculating." He leaned over to whisper, "It's in the genes."

"Like your cat vision."

"You were paying attention." The idea seemed to delight him. "Turn right, lover doll. That's another song, you know. Wait'll you see what I've done. You're gonna love it. Like I love you."

Darcy's blood ran cold. Could she reason with him? Should she try, or simply play along and hope that something, anything, might distract him long enough for her to escape?

Where was he taking her? Not the boarding-house. The park, maybe? No, not in this weather.

The gun jabbed her shoulder as she splashed through a pothole. She couldn't help jerking her head sideways when he attempted to kiss the hurt better.

Lightning flashed again, and she saw his mouth

turn down. "Don't do that! You're with me now. That makes you mine. If you want something, get it, that's what the old man says. So I got. You. Only thing I've ever wanted. And you want me, right? Say it, Darcy doll. You want me."

She swallowed the icy lump in her throat. "I want you."

"Then why haven't you asked how I did it?" He wiped his upper lip—not a good sign. "How I tricked her."

"You mean Hannah? I thought—"

"No, you didn't. You never think about me, do you? You let him touch you, but not me. Why not? Turn left. Don't you want to know?"

She struggled for a believable smile. "Yes, of course I do. I want to know everything. Tell me how clever you are, Ethan."

He blinked and stared at her. "You know my real name." He scooted as close as he could in Hannah's little Escort. "Was I wrong? Did you wonder about me?"

"Yes, I did. Often."

"You were curious, so you used your skills, and you dug. This is so cool. Turn left. You love me." A sly light appeared in his eyes. "You do love me, right?"

The gun tickled her neck. "I do," she said. "I love you."

Bending over, he nuzzled her jaw. This time, she held her breath and her position.

"The old man sent me to Oregon to learn about business conferences. That's how I found you. You looked at me from inside the TV, and you said, 'I want to be yours.' I'm sure that's what you told me. The old man said you didn't, but what does he know about love? Or my father? I mean, he sees sparkling lights and hears funny whispers and hides under his bed during thunderstorms."

Darcy ground her teeth so hard she thought they'd crack. "You're lucky you didn't inherit your father's tendencies."

"No, I'm like the old man. An opportunist with cat vision. I love wearing disguises, and I can act, too. And eavesdrop. You learn a lot by eavesdropping. I learned about Umer Lugo's plan to find me through you after I left the hospital. I hung around and listened at grandfather's window. That took balls, don't you think? Anyway, Lugo was going to hire a P.I. to find you because, me being obsessed and all, he figured I'd try to find you. He thought he could get to you first, and nail me when I made my move."

"That's very perceptive of you, Ethan."

"I know. Even better to follow Lugo around. Learn what he learns. Marlowe—man, I wish I could've killed him—does his job. Lugo flies to

Philly. But being Lugo and kinda paranoid, he goes all low-profile at a roadside motel, because, in case I'm onto him, which I am, would I think to look for him in a dive? He figures no, but ding, ding, Umer, I heard the chitter chatter at the old man's house. I know the plan. I plan to disrupt the plan. I hear Lugo and Marlowe talking in a Turkish restaurant. 'Here's where the Darcy doll lives, Lugo.' 'Great. Here's your money, Marlowe.' And I say, 'Here's your chance, Ethan.' Gotta kill Lugo first, though. Turn right."

Darcy's head swam. Insanity was merely a jumping-off point for this guy.

"So you discovered where I lived," she said with forced calm. "And then you discovered Hannah's boardinghouse."

"Right across from your house." He beamed at her. "Decided to get me a room." He made a knocking motion. "Tap, tap on the door. Big smile. Hannah stares. I stare back. She starts to laugh. Pulls me inside. Why I'm Cousin Arden's middle boy, aren't I? Am I? I keep smiling. She keeps talking." Using the tip of the gun, he tucked Darcy's hair behind her ear. "Opportunity, sugar pie. And fate. They were walking hand in hand for me that day. Now stop the car, and turn off the lights, 'cause, baby, we're here. Ethan's gonna love his Darcy doll tender tonight."

Darcy ordered herself to breathe. Because, God help her, she knew what would happen after the loving.

Ethan Lyons, aka Cristian Turner, was going to kill her.

Chapter Seventeen

The power was out. It must have been out for some time, because there was no sign of Hannah's sports-addicted husband at the boardinghouse.

Marlowe didn't care where Eddie'd gone, only where he was going two stairs at a time. Up to Cristian—no, scratch that—Ethan Lyons's room.

Once he'd relayed the description, Val's captain had made some angry calls to Los Angeles and come back with a name. Released on a day pass from a California mental hospital, Ethan Lyons, youngest grandson of Constantine Lyons, had pulled an R.J. Wilkie and vanished.

Somehow he'd posed as Hannah's cousin's son, though how he'd known to try remained a mystery. Bottom line, he'd done it. Slipped into the perfect disguise and worn it until the opportunity to snatch Darcy arose.

Fear was a lead weight in Marlowe's stomach. He reached Lyons's locked door, gave it a kick. When it didn't budge, he pulled his gun and shot the latch.

Lightning momentarily illuminated the room. Close on its heels, thunder rocked the old foundation.

In his mind, all Marlowe could see was Darcy.

Stuffing his gun away, he shone a flashlight over the walls. There were three store-bought Amish prints and one larger propped canvas that looked as if someone had mashed baby peas into it with his hands. So much for the budding Oklahoma artist.

Angling the beam downward, Marlowe spied a backpack and bulky duffel bag. He went for the pack first.

"You here, Marlowe?" Val's voice drifted up the staircase.

"In Lyons's room." Dumping the contents, he made a quick scan. Nothing but charcoal pencils, a bag of broken cookies and a sketchpad with dog-eared corners.

A light bobbed on the wall as he reached for the duffel.

"Comet's outside watching the front door." Val squatted next to him. "You got anything?"

"Props." Marlowe brought his eyes and his

flashlight up. "Wigs, mustache, putty. You said a pair of nurses recognized him from the hospital?"

"Apparently your guy's been doing volunteer work there. No idea why."

"Depends when he started." Marlowe identified the closet door, stood. "My guess is he signed on after Matilda was admitted. She saw him in the park the night I was shot."

"And the wigs and things?"

"He could have bought those things after she saw him. Or he decided not to bother with a disguise in the dark, figured the shadows would hide him well enough."

"Enough for what? So he could kill Darcy? If he's obsessed with her, why would he want to shoot her before he— Uh, well, you know."

Marlowe grimaced. "He wasn't gunning for Darcy that night. I'm the one he wanted. Jealousy, Val. I was with her. He wasn't."

"Except he missed. He had to run. And while running, slammed into the old woman, who probably got a real good look at him on that lighted path— Wait, what're you doing?"

This as Marlowe drew his gun and shot the closet door.

"It was locked."

Val stayed well back from him. "You're PO'd at me, aren't you?"

Kicking a mound of clothes away, Marlowe pointed his flashlight at the inside walls. "I haven't got time to be pissed off. But when I do, I will be. At you and me."

"Why at yourself? Holy—" Val stopped abruptly on the threshold, crossed his beam over Marlowe's. "There's a couple hundred pictures of Darcy in here."

The tightening in Marlowe's chest cinched his ribs, too, then climbed up into his throat. From the myriad photos, he could see that Lyons hadn't simply watched Darcy through the media, he'd stalked her with his own camera.

"How the hell close did you get?" he wondered aloud as his eyes landed on a shot of Darcy in a white lace bra and a matching thong. He shot a murderous look into the bedroom. "There has to be something. Go through his pockets, Val. I'll take the desk and dresser."

The elements outside continued to clash. No lights burned in the vicinity.

Keeping Darcy's face front and center in his mind, Marlowe searched the desk. He found a stack of paperbacks and two empty bags of chips.

The dresser was much the same. He was tugging on the third drawer when he noticed a scrap of newspaper taped to the mirror. There was a street name and number scribbled on it.

Snatching it free, he frowned. "Val, do you know Faldo Road?"

"Better than I want to. Amateur chemists cook up their street drugs in those houses."

Marlowe ran the address through his head. Why did he recognize it?

He heard a woman's voice talking about a house on Faldo Road. Whose voice? Not Darcy's.

It clicked with the next peal of thunder. Hannah Brewster.

Val emerged from the closet. "Did you say something?"

Marlowe ran the name again, and the memory attached to it. Hannah and her husband owned three properties. Two on this street and one on Faldo Road.

"Call Blydon." Marlowe checked his backup gun. "Tell him 927 Faldo. Tell him I'm going in."

"We're going in."

"You've been drinking, Val." Marlowe headed for the stairs, but Val trotted after him.

"I'm not drunk. And I swear to you, after tonight, I never will be again."

Shoving the clip in as he ran, Marlowe tucked his gun away. "Just so you know," he said, "Darcy comes first."

This time, he vowed, he wouldn't fail.

THE HOUSE WAS A WRECK, with crumbling plaster, broken fixtures and cobwebbed dust on every surface.

Darcy wouldn't have seen any of it if he hadn't lit candles every few feet. He nudged her at gunpoint up the ratty staircase to a second-floor bedroom. Once there, he leaned on the door to close it and used a taper to feed another dozen wicks.

The room smelled like old wood, roses and mold. Damp from the storm combined with the already high humidity to make the air almost unbreathable. Spying a window, Darcy immediately edged toward it.

"It's nailed shut, Darcy doll." He hummed while he lit the last of the candles. Then swung around, spread his arms and beamed with pride. "What do you think?" He indicated the walls where he'd stapled hundreds of photos of her. All doctored to include him. "Pictures of you right next to pictures of me. I went to Stanford, you know. Didn't graduate, but that's a long story involving a guy who thought Elvis sucked. Not sure if he left the hospital on foot or got wheeled down to cold storage. Oh, well."

Darcy eyed the door. "I, uh, see you've decorated Graceland style." The room was cluttered with heavy drapes and over-the-top furnishings.

His smile widened. "My grandmother bought me an Elvis suit, the white Las Vegas one, when I was five. She thought it was cute. I thought it was cool. My father thought it was possessed, but, hey, he's sick."

He set his lighter down, removed an iPod and cell phone from his scrubs. When he saw her watching him, he did a pirouette—gun in hand, Darcy noticed, though right then she was more interested in the phone.

"These aren't mine," he admitted, indicating the scrubs. "I had to borrow them so I could walk around without being noticed. I know the hospital, though. I started volunteering after I clocked the old lady. I figured you'd feel bad, seeing as you found her, and come to visit. Thought, hey, we could leave together."

His expression grew reptilian, chilling her blood. Madness, Darcy reflected, brought out the changeling element like nothing else.

"But you always brought Marlowe with you. I'd have killed him if I could. I killed the other P.I. tonight, but it's not the same. What was his name?"

Darcy worked her way toward the table. "Ivan Kazarov. He used to be a hit man."

"No kidding?" His face brightened. "The old man hired a hit man to find me? Must have been desperate. Kazarov, huh? I never knew who he was, only that he was after me. Duh. Didn't take a brain surgeon to figure that one out. But you and Marlowe screwed him up good. Wherever you went, he went. You thought he was the one grabbing you, but really, it was me. He was just there, skulking. That's called an ironic twist."

Picking up his iPod, he dropped it into a battery-operated dock and pressed Play. Elvis immediately poured from the speakers.

"'The Wonder Of You,'" Ethan intoned as he moved toward her, his eyes shining. "The wonder of us."

Darcy forced herself to breathe. She had to stay centered, talk to him, play along.

She fanned her face. "It's very hot up here, Ethan. Do you have anything cold to drink?"

"Lemonade."

Thunder rolled through the foundation and up the walls. Darcy heard the joists creak, saw the candles flutter.

"It's over here," he said. "In the red Thermos. No, the blue one. Red's full of kerosene."

Darcy's breath hitched. She masked it with a cough and a wave. "Dust. Old houses."

He picked up the Thermos, turned. "Are you sure you want me? You haven't kissed me."

She moved to the end of the table and smiled.

"I want to kiss you, Ethan, but well, actually, I'm a little shy."

"Were you shy with Marlowe?"

"Sometimes. Most times." Reaching behind her with one hand, she felt for the keypad on his cell phone. "I mean, he didn't matter, so I'm not sure shyness was ever an issue."

Instead of diminishing, his suspicion deepened. "I saw you kiss him more than once."

She thanked God as her thumb raced over the buttons that the next rumble of thunder was a protracted one. "I kiss lots of people. It doesn't mean anything." She sent him a deliberately flirtatious look. "Most times."

He gaped for a minute. "Oh, yeah? Wow."

Pick up, she willed silently. *Please pick up.* She had to let Marlowe know where she was, what was happening. And then she had to pray he'd make it here in time.

She accepted the lemonade Ethan handed her, and endured the light stroke of the gun barrel across her cheek. "I like your photos. They're very…flattering."

"I know. Okay, let's do it." He used his body to urge her toward a velvet-covered mattress in the corner.

Clamping down on her rising panic, she skimmed a finger over his jaw. "How did you happen to find Faldo Road?" she asked for—she hoped—Marlowe's benefit.

"It's Aunt Hannah's place." His own answer seemed to surprise him. "Did you hear that?" He laughed. "I called her Aunt Hannah. I'm still living the role. Don't you love it?"

"She's that kind of woman. Easy to know and like."

"Easy to dupe, you mean." He grinned. "She got arrested tonight. Cops going round the block—probably on account of you—saw her and Hancock mashing down the flowers at the front of your house, and they went to check it out. Guess her 'I'm the landlady' spiel didn't impress them. Hancock ran but she hung. Another squad car showed. It got really crazy, or so Uncle Eddie said. I didn't see any of it—I was too busy following you, Darcy doll—but Eddie did. Must've happened between innings. Anyway, he said they took her away." His eyes brightened. "So, do you wanna be on top or underneath?"

Darcy managed, barely, not to recoil when he kissed her hair. *Think,* she ordered herself. *Stall.*

"I, um…" Smiling, she set a hand on the wall. "I'm still feeling a little shy, Ethan. Tell me more while I work on that."

"More what?" He sounded impatient now, en route to angry.

"The gifts," she recalled suddenly. "You sent them, right? The dolls, the flowers, the jewelry? When I was in L.A."

The grin reappeared. "I sent you lots of things, but I liked the waterfall best. I saw it as you and me all twisted together, hot, then frozen in place forever. It is us, Darcy doll, or it will be. Hot and steamy now, streaking toward forever. It should have happened in Atlantic City. You were so pretty that night in your strapless dress and red shoes. So perfect." His features clouded. "So sneaky. I was telling Elvis how really great it had all gone down. I was thanking him for helping me, and then I heard the door opening and when I came back into the room, you were gone. Did you get confused?"

"Yes," she said quickly. "I did. I lost my bearings. Must have been the chloroform."

She knew he was watching her face so she smiled again and touched his cheek. "Chemicals are unpredictable things, Ethan. People react to them in different ways."

"So you weren't running back to Marlowe like I thought?"

A resounding bang from the lower level cut off Darcy's response.

"You here, Bert?" a voice shouted up the stairs. "It's Ernie. I got the shipment. Uzis and Lugers, boxes of 'em. Been practicing with one of the new models. You could shoot the wings off a fly at fifty yards." A disgusted snort reached them. "Aw, what's this crap? You're burning candles? When'd you turn into a girl? Maybe I need to shoot you, huh?"

Darcy checked a desire to bolt. "He sounds big."

"Bert!" The name was a snap now.

Her fingers curled into Ethan's arm, but he twisted free, began blowing out candles. "Help me. No, wait!" He whipped his gun around. "I can shoot him first."

Darcy thought fast. "Dark's better than light. Gives us the advantage."

"Yeah, dark's good." He used the gun to gesture. "You blow. I'll watch the door."

She went straight for the candelabra on the table.

She heard footsteps in the corridor. "Crissakes, Bert, you got flowers up here, too? What kind of sissy you turning into?"

Instead of extinguishing the candles, Darcy grabbed the brass holder with both hands, and, using it like a bat, she brought it down hard on Ethan's arm. He grunted and dropped the gun just as the door burst open and Marlowe flew inside.

Two others might have followed. Darcy couldn't be sure because Ethan had knocked her sideways, and now there was chaos everywhere.

"No!" Ethan screamed, then snarled and dove into the corner.

Someone shoved Darcy, but she spun around, caught hold of a T-shirt.

"It's me," Marlowe said quietly.

"I know." She shook him. "He's has kerosene. And a gun."

As if on cue, a bullet ricocheted off the table next to him.

"Go." Marlowe pushed her toward the door. "Backup's coming."

"Backup's here." She recognized Val's voice.

Another shot glanced off the edge.

"You tricked me," Ethan cried.

He fired off successive shots. Before anyone could move, the Thermos exploded. An enormous ball of flame erupted. Kerosene sprayed everywhere, and with it thousands of orange sparks.

"Comet!" Marlowe caught the informant as he toppled into his arms.

"He hit me in the shoulder. Stings," Comet said through his teeth.

Ethan fired two more shots.

Marlowe pushed Darcy down with a hand on her shoulder. He held her there.

Choking smoke filled the room. Marlowe's fingers wrapped around her neck as he crouched. "Take Comet and get out of here."

He held her stare until she nodded. Then he kissed her and vanished. Not into the fire. She had to believe he wouldn't go that far.

Flames flowed across the floor like lava. They rose up the wall to the ceiling, swept along the rafters, then rolled back down.

Smoke surrounded them, a noxious black cloud of it. She heard more shots—two, three, four of them. They seemed to come from every direction.

Comet wheezed as she helped him stand. "Eyes are spotty," he grunted. "Arm's going numb. Which way's out?"

Darcy couldn't see the hall. She could only go on memory.

She heard someone yelp as another bullet whizzed past.

"Val?" Darcy waved at the smoke. "Is that you? Are you all right?"

A hand appeared as he hauled himself up. "He hit me."

She got Val around his waist, felt him sag against her.

The fire spit embers at them as the flames crept closer.

"Get out of here, Darcy," Marlowe hissed in her ear.

"I'm trying," she said and, coughing, got Val's arm around her. "Where's Ethan?"

"I lost him. Go. Stay ahead of me."

He took Val's weight, left Comet to her.

She couldn't see any better in the hallway, but at least she could breathe.

They were halfway down the wide staircase when a fresh round of bullets peppered them from above.

Marlowe spun, crouched and fired back. Darcy reached for Val's arm. Or started to.

The movement happened so fast, it didn't register. One minute, she was beside Val; the next, someone darted past, grabbing her and hauling her down the remaining stairs.

She landed on something soft, but only for a moment. Ethan whipped his forearm around her throat and yanked her back against him.

"Cat in the dark, Darcy doll." He jammed his gun under her chin, cocked the hammer. "I've got three bullets left. One for you, one for me." His voice quivered. He snatched the gun away, pointed it three steps up. "And one for your lover."

"Ethan, don't." She pried on his wrist. "He's not—"

"He is. The King told me to be suspicious in his song, but I ignored him."

"Let her go, Lyons." Marlowe lowered his own gun.

Ethan gave a bitter laugh, coughed at the

smoke that was slinking down the staircase. "Well, okay, I'll do that, then." He raised his voice. "Either of you move, and loverboy here gets a bullet between the eyes. Oh, wait, he's going to get one anyway. My mistake. Feel free to move."

Darcy couldn't see Marlowe's face. She couldn't even see the staircase. But she knew Ethan could.

"Don't," she said when his firing arm vibrated.

"Shut up, Darcy doll. Your lover can send you a postcard from hell."

She didn't know what else to do. Standing beside him, she couldn't spike him, and if she went for his solar plexus he'd shoot. So she sucked in a breath, shouted at Marlowe and, twisting sideways, sank her teeth into Ethan's wrist.

He jerked and jumped backward, the gun firing as he did. The arm holding her tightened and he made a garbled sound. Then, as if his bones had dissolved, he slithered to the ground.

Darcy freed herself before he could drag her down. She almost lost her balance, but Marlowe was there to steady her. He shielded her with his body—but not before a large portion of the ceiling detached and landed in a shower of sparks on the floor below.

Everything had become surreal and Darcy couldn't discern reality any longer. Around her she heard shouts and sirens and saw a dizzying array of lights. Their strobing tempo seemed to bring all the action to slow motion. Behind her she heard the roar of the fire and above her, the underlying growl of thunder. Clearing her eyes, she saw angry orange and blue flames and wicked zaps of lightning.

Firefighters and rescue workers came and went. At one point, she saw Val tumble onto the lawn, followed by Comet. Then she noticed Ethan Lyons, strapped onto a gurney, jerking convulsively as consciousness returned.

Five feet away, she saw Marlowe watching her while he talked to Val's captain.

It could have been an hour, it might have been five. The house was a raging inferno; then, in a snap, it was charred rubble. The storm moved on, leaving the smell of wet wood and eerie tendrils of black smoke in its wake.

A gray car rolled to a halt at the curb while the firefighters were packing up their hoses. Darcy noticed it, but her focus remained on Marlowe as he walked toward her.

She would have met him halfway if her legs hadn't felt like straw. She leaned on the fire truck instead and hoped he'd get there before she collapsed.

When he caught her hand and tugged, she summoned a weary smile. "I gather—"

Whatever she'd been about to say died as his mouth came down on hers in a kiss that electrified every beleaguered nerve in her body.

Nothing penetrated until he raised his head to stare down at her.

Wrapping her arms around his neck, she let the horror fade into the background and amusement stir. "You really know how to do that, don't—"

He cut her off again, this time with a gentler kiss that took her on a carousel ride of pure pleasure.

"Excuse me."

A man's voice slowly worked its way in. Darcy had an impression of authority combined with advanced age. Then she spied the man speaking and, fisting her hands in Marlowe's hair, tugged.

He looked frail, almost birdlike, sitting in his wheelchair. Neither smiling nor frowning, he waited patiently for their attention. Once he had it, his ice-blue eyes began to glitter.

"Ms. Nolan, Mr. Marlowe, allow me to introduce myself. My name is Constantine Lyons."

Chapter Eighteen

"Are you serious?" Darcy's boss was elated. "You met the old man himself? Kiddo, Constantine Lyons is the Howard Hughes of the heavy-duty tool industry...."

If only she knew, Marlowe reflected late the next day. That she probably never would was something he chose to let Darcy deal with alone. He had enough on his plate, juggling Val, Blydon, the Lyons's new family lawyer and his own conflicted emotions.

"He won't serve a day in prison," Val predicted as the last of Ethan Lyons's belongings were bagged and tagged at the boardinghouse. "Old Conly and his pal, the California Supreme Court judge, will see to that. On the plus side, he won't see the free light of day again, either."

"All kinds of prisons out there," Marlowe remarked. "Long as he ends up in one of them."

"That's awfully big of you, considering he tried

to kill you and would have killed Darcy if you hadn't shot him first."

"Murder, suicide." Marlowe regarded the now locked door of room four. "That was the plan. Both of them dead. Together forever."

"You think the family can hush it up this time?"

"Don't know. It's been done before—several times apparently—with Ethan, his brother and his father. Keep it in the family, no cops, no media, no fuss. In this case, only Lugo and his backup, Kazarov, were in the old man's loop. The rest of the family was oblivious."

"To Ethan's escape or his obsession?"

"Both, if Constantine's telling the truth. And at this point, he's got no reason to lie."

"Yeah, well, money may talk, old friend, and certain legal eagles might listen, but this time around, there are two dead bodies and a certain newsmagazine editor who's chomping at the bit to be the next Woodward or Bernstein. We also have a snitch with a hole in his shoulder— although that part's more my fault than Lyons's. I let Comet ride with me from the hospital. Man, I've never had an informant show me a tenth the loyalty that guy showed you. You should take him on as your assistant."

Marlowe gave a small laugh. "Maybe I will."

"And if you're planning to expand, you might

also consider taking on a junior partner, one whose AA meetings begin tonight."

Marlowe started down the stairs. "Sick of the cop life, Val?"

"Sick of, not cut out for—take your pick. How's Darcy doing? Last I saw, she had your landlady draped all over her, sobbing about an outraged husband, a missing tenant and a flip-flop she still can't find. Whatever that means."

"It means she was having an affair with Hancock and using Darcy's place for her low-rent rendezvous. Hannah didn't quite make it out the first time. That was the night Darcy and I found her in a closet with a garrote."

"Excuse me?"

"Think dominatrix, and if you're smart, don't take it any further. The next problem occurred when she lost one of her trademark flip-flops. In Darcy's house, she thought. It fell out of a bag, so she didn't realize it was gone at first. Eventually, she sent Hancock back in to get it. When he couldn't find it, he started searching the bushes. Darcy showed up, he hid, used the cat as a diversion and managed to slip away unnoticed. The third time, last night, it was the cops rather than Darcy who showed. She got caught, Hancock took off, and Eddie discovered the pitfalls of being a couch potato."

"The stuff that goes on in sleepy neighborhoods." Val shook his head. "Not that this relates, but we found Hickey."

"Performing?"

"Rehabbing. He checked into a private hospital in Queens while you were in Atlantic City." His brows went up when Marlowe's cell phone began playing Clapton's "Beautiful Tonight." "Well, hey, that's a pleasant switch. Any particular blond-haired, blue-eyed reason?"

He cast a meaningful look at Darcy, who'd apparently ditched both her landlady and editor and was currently leaning on the side of her car. Waiting for him, Marlowe hoped, though he was still too twisted up inside to think about where any of this might lead.

"Does this new ring tone mean you've told her about Lisa?"

When Marlowe merely shot him a look, he nodded. "Got it. None of my business. On that note, M, I'll ride off into the sunset and my meeting. When you're thinking with your head again, give some consideration to the junior partner thing. I know I blew it with the DMV photo, but come on, Ethan Lyons and Cristian Turner look a hell of a lot alike."

"Yeah, except for the part of Lyons's left earlobe that a Rottweiler mangled long before the last DMV picture of Turner was taken."

"I'll remember that for future comps. Solution's in the details." Val raised his voice and his hand to Darcy. "I'm thinking dinner tomorrow night, darling. Any restaurant you want. My treat."

She pushed upright, eyes twinkling. "Oh, never be that open-ended with me, Val. I have expensive taste, and I happen to know you're still working on a raft of old IOUs."

"McDonald's it is. Well, wish me luck, people. I've never stood up and told my story before."

Darcy waited until he was gone to stroll over and hook her arms around Marlowe's neck. "Curious as I am to know what he means, I'm going to set that and all other questions aside in favor of a single pressing one."

Drawing her firmly against him, Marlowe looked into her incredible blue eyes. "And that is?"

She brought her mouth within an inch of his to whisper, "How many times do you plan on making love to me tonight?"

His eyes gleamed. "Depends."

"On?"

"Your stamina." And as he covered her mouth with his, Marlowe felt the pain inside him begin to slide away.

MIDNIGHT CAME AND WENT. With a sprinkling of stars overhead and the moon glowing like an enormous white pearl, Darcy brought a bottle of wine to her back porch, sat next to Marlowe on the step and poured.

Smiling smugly, she tapped her glass to his. "Remember, this break was your idea, not mine—should the question of stamina happen to arise."

"Yeah, well, I'm a little out of practice these days."

"Could have fooled me." Turning slightly, she played with his hair. "Do you want to talk?"

"I'm working on it."

Because she knew he was, she helped him out. "Who came up with the Bert-and-Ernie diversion on Faldo Road, and did you hear any of the conversation between Ethan and me before you got there?"

Marlowe's lips twitched. "That was Comet's idea. Guess he likes *Sesame Street*. As for what I heard, I picked up while Lyons was telling you the place belonged to his Aunt Hannah."

"Which you'd already figured out, and I'm really glad you had since he was pushing me toward his idea of a Graceland bed at the time." She swirled her wine. "You know, for a moment while he was strapped down, I almost felt sorry for him. No one could want to be that insane."

"That obsessed. That dangerous."

"I know, but really, Marlowe, according to his grandfather, Ethan's been in and out of psychiatric hospitals since he was thirteen—which, on a side note, accounts for the gaps in the gifts he sent me. He'd been released on a twelve-hour pass the day he escaped. I mean, get real, what kind of doctor authorizes a pass for someone as sick as that?"

"One who likes money."

"Then for his sake, I hope he's got a huge stash of it, because by the time Elaine gets through with this story, said doctor will be stripped of his credentials and possibly forced to take refuge in Panama." Laughing, she tickled his ribs. "Is that a grin I see on your supersexy face?"

"I just had a picture of Lyons's shrink sitting next to your former coworker on that Panamanian flight."

"Oh, I think Trace's story is a little different than Ethan's. I truly believe Trace could be helped if he'd bother to try. Wouldn't make him a more likeable person, but a few less neuroses and a little anger management couldn't hurt." She regarded the moon. "It *was* Trace I saw at the hospital, you know. Elaine said he came to her place to talk, and wound up putting put his hand through a wall. Broke three knuckles and his thumb. His hand'll be in a cast for weeks."

Leaning back on one elbow, Marlowe let his eyes roam the small garden. "In the cop world, your tone would be described as gleefully malicious."

"Which I can only justify by claiming that the shock of this nightmare hasn't worn off yet."

"Would another round of wild sex upstairs speed that process along?"

"Might." But she sighed and, leaning over, drew a circle on his chest. "Vacation would be better. Or…" she raised her eyes "…a bedtime story."

He sipped his wine. "Nice segue, Darcy. Wish I had a nice story for you in return, but the only one I know doesn't end with happily ever after."

She kissed his chin. "Would it help if I told you that Comet's a very chatty man, and he knows a great deal more about your past than you probably realize?"

He stared at her in mild suspicion. "You talked to Comet about my past?"

"No, he talked to me while we were driving to the hospital. Just blurted it out in one long, rambling sentence."

"He told you about Lisa."

She nodded.

Marlowe's gaze shifted to the grass. "She was five years old when a sniper's bullet killed her.

Elizabeth—her mother—and I had been divorced for four years. But I had every weekend with Lisa from the time we split up. I took her to an amusement park one Saturday night. Shouldn't have because I'd been threatened earlier in the week. But she wanted to go, and her birthday was three days away."

"Little girls know how to get around their daddies," Darcy said gently, and brushed his cheek.

"Lisa was alive when we went to the park and dead when we left. The guy who'd threatened me earlier that week must have followed us. He was aiming for me, but he missed and killed her. I remember screams and sirens and flashing lights. I remember swearing I'd get him. I remember the guilt eating away at me and not caring if it ate me up."

"Did you catch him?" Darcy asked.

"Oh, yeah." A trace of a smile crossed Marlowe's lips. "I cornered him seven months later. He shot, then I shot. He got me in the shoulder. I got him in the chest. He was dead before he hit the ground."

Darcy waited for the rest. When he didn't continue, she ventured, "He was dead, but…?"

"It didn't help. It didn't change what was. It didn't do what I wanted it to do, what I needed it to do, what I'd somehow expected it to do."

"It didn't bring her back."

"No, it only made me shut down. I think now I was right on the edge of no way back when Lugo called me. I was tempted to say, 'Screw you,' buy a ticket to Margaritaville and leave it at that."

"But instead you took the job and screwed up my life."

He laughed a little, moved the hair from her cheek. "That pretty much sums it up. With one important omission."

"Which is?"

Setting a finger under her chin, he brought her mouth to his. "I love you, Darcy. Didn't think I would. I didn't think I could. But I do. Suddenly Margaritaville's lost its appeal."

"And the guilt?"

"Still there, but manageable, and I'm guessing normal. I want to go forward. I want the future to matter. I want you to be my future, or a very large part of it."

"Future's kind of a scary word to me," she began, but he pushed her onto her back and kissed the objection away.

When he lifted his head, she laughed. "So much for drawing out the moment. Before I wind up senseless and tripping on emotion, I guess I'll say I love you, too. Which still sort of amazes me when I think about it, because while I make friends easily, I hardly ever get involved. You snuck in, Marlowe, and I have to tell you, that scares the hell out of me."

"Fair enough. Means we're staring off on even ground."

"Oh, good." She nipped his bottom lip. "Now, exactly where would that even ground be? Here or New York?"

He grinned. "I'm flexible."

"In that case, we'll flip a coin." Moving her mouth to his ear, she gave him a gentle bite and whispered, "Later."

* * * * *